This book is dedicated to my mum, Thembeka, and my wife, Nolita, who have both been the power behind my work. I give a whole world of thanks to the women and activists who have tirelessly fought for the rights of women who have been deprived because of their gender, not by choice.

Vuyisile Louis Poti was born in Tinis Location, Fort Beaufort, South Africa. He is a mental health author who has worked his entire life as a registered mental health nurse, registered general nurse and an occupational health nurse (Employee Assistance Practitioner) in South Africa and England.

Graduated from Fort Hare University in 1991, with a major in Nursing Science, psychiatry, community health nursing, and midwifery, where he met and married his college sweetheart of 34 years and still counting.

Mental Health has been his subject of interest and that's what strongly drove him to produce his first book, *The Quotable Quotes* Dementia refined, which was published in 2021. His quest to stretch his wings has led us to Nikita. Enjoy…

Vuyisile Louis Poti

NIKITA…YOU DARE NOT!

AUSTIN MACAULEY PUBLISHERS™

LONDON • CAMBRIDGE • NEW YORK • SHARJAH

A CIP catalogue record for this title is available from the British Library.

ISBN 9781035816910 (Paperback)
ISBN 9781035816927 (Hardback)
ISBN 9781035816934 (ePub e-book)

www.austinmacauley.com

First Published 2024
Austin Macauley Publishers Ltd®
1 Canada Square
Canary Wharf
London
E14 5AA

Table of Contents

Introduction

The Unknown World

7/10 times this world is explored through curiosity, planned/unplanned research work, investigative procedures and others. This can be more fun one could imagine and more interesting and enjoyable to the learner who bears no permanent attachment to the experience. Not knowing what is waiting for you on the other side can be a daunting experience, exciting, scary and anxious moments.

The main aim is to satisfy the curiosity, to learn and to know more about the situation, to find a solution or a cure, to prove a point or to agree to disagree. Life is a game, play it right and fair—you are a winner; play it wrong and you are as good as dead. This is not a puzzle; this is a real-life situation. What goes in sufferers' minds is beyond belief. The onlooker might think, this is an exaggeration, or something might have been horribly gone wrong.

She was only thirty-two when her life took an undesirable turning point. She had only one person to turn to, only one person who could have possible answers to her questions. Why now, why not earlier on? Those were some of the questions no one could answer except her mum. "I grew up with parents, two very loving parents and a sister I cherish and now I am stripped all that fun." Those were the cries no one could bear. She did not know where she would go from that point and how her life would be after her meeting with her mum. She was angry at both, and she needed some answers and she needed them quick.

In the midst of trying to re-root herself, the unthinkable happened. As if she did not have enough problems she was diagnosed with auditory hallucinations. Hearing commanding voices was not in her script at that moment but there was nothing she could do about it. "Why me!" She screamed. "Why am I being punished for the sins I did not commit," she continued in tears.

"You are the chosen one, make them pay Nikita," the voices spoke louder and louder in her ears.

"Who are you?" She asked anxiously.

"We are the defenders of the defenceless," they continued.

"I am not defenceless," she snapped.

"We know, ha-ha-ha," they laughed and then disappeared.

"Go away and never come back, you devil," she shouted and sat down holding her head tight.

Social Support

Lack of social support could prove to increase the risk of vulnerability or detachment to the psychological assistance one may be having. Strong social ties may lessen or inhibit the psychological trauma a person might be having.

"Bad things often happening enough, early enough or sufficiently severe can drive us mad with or without a genetic predisposition." Simon McCarthy Jones (2017)

At risk—that's what we refer to the sufferers. You suffer, you lose your identity, you are amongst the group, the diabetics, the schizophrenics, the hyper/hypotensive, the self-harmers, the bipolars, the OCD's and so on. You name it, they are labelled with it. They are referred to as cases. That individuality has gone forever.

How many times have people been rescued from suicidal attempts, how many have been lost through the successful attempts? How many family members have been on the verge of mental breakdown themselves crying out and devastatingly pleading, "We care about you, please don't," he /she could have been saved, he/she has been failed by the system, the coroner has ruled this and that, the police has ruled out foul play and later on, "new evidence has led to new investigations." That is the common trait in our societies.

Problems originates from what I call IFS. This is a combination of factors, the triangle which has an impact on human lives, individuals, families and the society.

IFS as the name suggests starts from individual problems which becomes a family burden and goes beyond to be a societal concern. This is not the end to the beginning of problems but can be blown out of proportion as more questions need to be asked and the "what ifs" of IFS becomes a national or even an international concern.

The Loop

This is not as open and accessible as we think. There are cases (as they are commonly called) which are not accounted for. The unreported indoor activities mostly familial are unknown. This may be due to cultural beliefs / practices or fear factor. These cases are very difficult to deal with because when they come into the open, they have already complicated and need specialist attention or extreme rehabilitation. They can prove to be more costly than one could imagine.

The System

As much as the system is doing its utmost best to curb the situation there are still notable islets who do not attempt to step up to their plates and thus dragging the system down to failure. The war is far from over. The cases are mounting and the people we trust are letting us down big time.

Trauma

The word trauma originates from the Greek word "wound." Talking about wounds, the existence or non-existence of emotional trauma in the olden days is unbelievably amazing. One may argue it was existent but blocked. This is a strange world, when I listened to my family members telling stories about their boyhood stick battles, they boast about healed wounds as if they were trophies. They wore them with pride. They will go about identifying them, this one is from so and so and this one I got from so and so.

That was intriguing, but to think about it now, this was assault and on a more serious note these were head injuries they were talking about. That was emotional distress suppressed. I have heard people boasting by walking the Wall of China or by seeing the Pyramids of Egypt but not boasting about trauma they suffered is rather weird.

"The hurly-burly of clinical work makes life very busy. There were a lot of people out there to listen to who had experienced psychological trauma and the field was moving fast, with new discoveries in neuroscience making the connections between our inner wiring and our thinking patterns, emotions and behaviours." Turnbull (2011)

The strains, the stresses and stressors never mind the physical trauma we encounter pushes us to extreme limits and drives us around the bend. Psychological trauma increases the risk of instability and makes one vulnerable to other stresses. The experiences we go through, the challenges we encounter have a great impact in our lives, be it positive or negative. Most of us experience trauma of some kind in our lives but how we perceive it is a different story.

The mind is a complex machine.

Nikita was not different, she had flesh and blood but was thick skinned. Her mind set was to deal with issues as they come. Can you prioritise trauma—physical trauma yes, but emotional trauma, help me out, but I think she was capable of doing that in her mind? The impact of the incident hit her hard but it's the after-effects that grinded her slowly. The fear of freedom, the eagerness to erase this trauma and get away from its after-effects, was what was on her mind.

People forgive but do not forget, that's the fact. But the problem with emotional trauma, is that it keeps coming to you. It never heals and it can complicate to something else.

Voices

Voices are waiting to speak to you. They know your

name, they know where you live, they know your loved ones, they know your enemies, they despise opposition, they hate to be ignored, they like to be dominant, they are harmless but can drive you to be harmful, they are influential and very powerful.

The experience is implausible, unreasonable and real. What does it mean to hear voices?

How does it feel to hear voices? Are they really real? Are they meaningful messengers?

Why do they pick on certain individuals? Can they be revengeful? What are they trying to tell us?

Voice hearing is predominantly portrayed as an unambiguous harbinger of madness caused by a broken brain, an unbalanced mind, biology gone wild!

Could bad childhood have bearing on hearing voices?

Impact on Self

The mind is a resourceful multi-departmental hierarchy. One department fails and the whole organisation goes down. The experiences we go through, the challenges we are encountering, have a great impact on our lives be it negative or positive, building or destroying. We all experience trauma of a kind in our lives but how we receive it is very different. Gender has nothing to do with the results, there are weaker men than women and vice-versa.

Critics may argue men are stronger than women but having said so, one might consider that there is a vast difference between a physical and psychological trauma and physique has little or no bearing on the results. Culture—what leads to the end results depend on how we perceive the impact of trauma in our lives. Suffering childhood trauma increases the risk of mental instability and thus making one vulnerable to other stress disorders and even more than one has bargained for.

I am becoming to look silly; I know. Since 06h30 this morning I have been seeing ghosts. They are silent, but the message is clear. I do not know how to explain this, they are not forcing me to do things, but are telling me things and by the looks of things are expecting my reaction either verbally, physically or otherwise. I am not worried about them, but they are disturbing. They tell me things about other people, not bad things, but the way they are conveyed to me is very strange. They look and sound real, I must admit and very difficult to ignore. I am tired emotionally and I think physically as well now.

I want to see my doctor as soon as possible. Am I still on the dosage of tablets or has there be anything added to what I have been taking? This is a strange feeling, like something new has entered my system. I may be wrong, may be just mere speculation but I am curious to know what causes this. Do I sound silly? I am really so sorry to put you in this, I know this is not your problem. I wish this goes away very soon and never come back.

The next minute…

As if I was not there, she blanked out completely. She started talking to herself and as time went on it became a two-way conversation talking to the so called "Ghost." This was interesting and somewhat intense. Sometimes I could hear her apologising and the next minute confronting the opposition and shaking hands, laughing loudly, nodding, embracing.

This was no ordinary experience; this was extra-ordinary. I was a very inquisitive spectator but did not want to spoil the party. This was becoming weird, because by the sound of things she was talking to one or two people as she was looking to different directions when exchanging words.

And then…

Silence. A very long deafening silence.

Impact on Others

This is disturbing to the onlooker, but people must try to approach this situation positively rather than challenging the existence of voices as people usually do. This is a very scary and devastating situation. It deprives families of their loved ones, of their dads and mums, brothers and sisters and significant others. Voices can be dangerous to both the sufferer and people around him/her. That sometimes depend on the message being conveyed and the receipt of that message on the other end.

Making a Statement

This is insane. How could they do this to me? So, all these years, my entire life, I have been living under an umbrella shelter of lies. You are the best thing that ever happened to me, you are the best daughter in the whole universe, those birthdays, those presents, those speeches. Why, why, why? She screamed, banging the table hard with her bare fists. Were all these lies? This is not on, and this is far from over.

I need answers, and I need answers right now or the hell will break loose. Not another Virginia Woolf nor another

Brian Wilson. I'd rather be a human shield—I will fight until the end. Call it cruelty, call it vengeance, who cares. This is my war! It's payback time. There are things I have forgotten in my life, deliberately sometimes, there are things I have just ignored but this, this…is beyond forgiveness (she shook her head).

The reaction beat everyone. Let the sleeping dogs lie young lady, whispered an old man passing by. Let the bygones be bygones is not going to work old man, replied his compatriot. This is fire, inextinguishable fire. Good luck to whoever she is referring to. It does not take a genius to realise that somewhere, somehow, someone is going to pay heavily, she really meant that; mark my words. I have been in this world long enough to know the difference between a threat and a promise.

You have heard it from the horse's mouth, a reliable source (shall I say). This is a promise, never to be broken. I wish it was marriage—those things break easily these days.

Social Stigma

Social stigma can be related to other characteristics including gender, sexuality, race, religion and culture. Stigma includes negative attitudes or discrimination against someone based on a distinguishing characteristic such as a mental health condition or disability.

Societies differ, people differ, cultures differ and so are beliefs. Similarities are not ruled out, but culture and beliefs play a pivotal role in in determining how people behave.

People tend to move away from their places of birth but running away does not solve the problem as in some cases one might be moving away from the pot and run straight into a burning fire. Of course, there are times when it is therapeutic to move away from a stressful situation and get a breather. Having said so there are situations that will never go away and have to be dealt with one way or another.

There are things you cannot change in life, but it does comfort sometimes to settle the scores.

Nikita was in a complex, complicated situation and she needed a strong cocktail of assistance, fast.

Try this one for size.

Profiling the Profiler

Nikita was a genius. She was manipulative, split decision masterminder, calm, had innocent looks and very dangerous. To confuse the situation more she was very seductive, a blinder to the weaklings. She was well known to her closest friends for personality change andmood swings. (Which was not a common denominator when she was with the others) She had good timing and liked to detail her actions.

She was a charming character.

She has learnt a lot from the master. They could just admit, she wastoo good a player for this game. She knew them and their moves like she knew the back of her hand. It will take a genius to catch this girl. They thought she was one step ahead of them, she was taught that one is not enough. His master was too smart, a genius in the making. He did not do things to perfection; he even inspired the opposition.

Take a look at Bob…

The comparison of the General to Bob is one of those unfamiliar coincidences, which always spices up the experiences braced with enthusiasm and dedication.

Carol and her in-laws sat down, and, in their meeting, they decided to do a surprise birthday party for Bob. This was kept as a secret fromBob (so they thought). Bob's birthday was nearing, and preparations were quietly done under his nose and things were going according to plan until…

Carol received a call from one of her employers booking her to cover a long day shift. She did what most of us do, she said yes and later realised, actually I cannot do that shift. The date of that shift was on Bob's birthday for God's sake.

"Oh, sugar," she said loudly. "What have I done?"

"What?" Bob asked.

"I have just agreed to do a shift at Glebe House Nursing Home and in reality, I cannot do."

"Why not?" Bob insisted.

"It is your birthday, darling. I can't."

She thought she could get awaywith it if she cancelled the shift but with Bob insisting that she go to work and they can celebrate later, she had no option and was forced to spill the beans. Bob was not going away and with his stubbornness, he was complicating the situation. Bob was doing nothing wrong, just making her wife a priority.

"Bob," she said with her posh voice and gave him that smile that forces him to say "yes" to everything.

"Yes love." Bob was all ears.

"Promise me please not to say this to anyone," she continued.

"Go on, I am listening," Bob said a bit anxious about this suspense.

"I want you to behave as if I never told you this," Carol was trying to compose herself.

"Told me what my love?" Bob was becoming more anxious.

"We planned to do a surprise party for you tomorrow. You weresupposing not to know this. So, when we go to your mum tomorrow, as if you know nothing and go with the flow. Most important, "be surprised." Come on love, I am not asking too much, am I?"

He was in one of those situations you say no, you might miss supper (if you know what I mean), and who would like to miss a turkey on a Christmas day.

As stunned as he was, he had no option but to stick to his wife's plan. Such is the beauty of marriage. "In sickness and in health, till deathdo us apart." Whichever way you look at it, it is binding in all angles. Such is life, it has its own frills, twists and turns.

Chapter 1
Down the Road...

"Get up and be ready," was the newly formed tune by the Napego sisters remembering their dad as he always prompted them every morning. Not that they were the lazy bunch, but he was the earliest bird ready for its first worm of the morning.

"I bet he would be sleeping today, he never liked hospital appointments," said Nikita.

"Not particularly hospital appointments but needles and knives," added Tamara.

"Actually, not needles and knives but he did not want to be put to sleep in case he would not wake up," said their mum entering the kitchen.

"Oh, sorry mum, did we wake you up," apologised Nikita.

"Who would not with all that jubilation, what was that song again?"

"Get up and be ready or someone else is going to catch your worm by Nikita Napego," answered Tamara.

"I wanted her to be a singer and she chose to be a medic," said her mum with no regrets.

"Are you ready mum?" Nikita asked.

"This seems to be the theme of the day, give me ten, I will be there," she went to her bedroom.

"No haste," said Tamara, "the lady of the day. I am happy that I do not feel right, have you ever had that feeling," she continued.

"Like father like daughter, knives and needles," laughed Nikita.

"The apple does not fall away from its tree, so they say, are you ready to go girls?" Mum added.

"I am not scared ok, let's not talk about this now."

"Look at me, we are in the same boat, I will be undergoing the same procedure and to add more I will be first," said Nikita hugging her little sister and taking their bags to the car.

They made their way to the city hospital in a happy mood trying to cheer up Tamara and they were received with almost the same atmosphere in hospital.

Chapter 2
There Comes Trouble...

Tamara's appointment with the surgeons did not go very well. The laboratory results revealed that Nikita was not eligible to help her sister with the bone marrow as they were not compatible. I did not catch that first but as the surgeons asked more questions, it became clear to me that I have some answers to give here not only to them but to my children as they anxiously wanted to know why.

The medical team was wise enough to take me aside when they got the results. I was shocked. I am not medically literate, but I think I should have known and expected this could happen, this is not a rocket science. God has his own ways of revealing things, I told myself. Be strong you've got to deal with this, I tried to pump myself up. I think the girls could read on my face that there was something troubling me, and I could not shake it off.

The medical team, seeing how distraught I was on hearing those results decided to deal with the girls so as to ease the pressure on me. Did it help? Yes and no. It gave her a little breathing space to think how she was going to deal with them but what came after was heartbreaking. I prayed and prayed. I heard footsteps like a horse galloping coming stronger towards my bedroom. I closed my eyes and told myself, this is it.

She stormed into my bedroom. She was very, very angry. There was, no knock no greetings and she just stared at me. I never saw that side of Nikki before. You knew this, didn't you. Before I even I even said a word, she snapped.

"And you continued to make me a damn fool. I trusted you and you betrayed my trust. I gave you all my heart and what did you do, you make me sick..." and off she went. She was shaking and clinching her teeth and her fists. I was lost for words, heartbroken but not angry. I knew she was hurting.

I never thought in my entire life that I would for even one millisecond stand accused by my own children. This was humiliation at its worst. I felt that someone was peeling off unhealed wounds. It was a very slow unendurable pain, a permanent scar. This was no ordinary pain. She loved and trusted her 'father.' She was hurting, visibly hurt. I was hurting inside too; this was killing me. I was not sweating; this was not a sweat—these were the rivers of Babylon.

I thought I was strong. Surprisingly, Nikita wanted to know the whole story. They were both staring at me, and I think I had no choice but to reveal what happened. I tried to comfort them and reassured them that this is not going to change anything, it will pass but it's going to take some time. The most important thing is to stick together as a family, love each other as we always did and be strong.

I did not want to say too much in case I overstep as I was becoming more emotional. Tamara was confused. I think she did not know who to start with comforting, her big sister or her mother because we were both crying. This was a very sad moment for all of us. Sit down please, I invited them.

How it all happened…

Your dad dubbed the night "the night of the owls." We laughed at that because we juggled where we were going to spend the night. We had so many options and we picked this one place to spend the night. We were so upbeat about it; it was highly recommended, and its rating spoke for itself. You never argue with five stars, do you? Everything was set, or shall I say the stage was set for the biggest night of our lives. We had never been out for a while because of work commitments, ups and downs of life, moving to our new house, renovations and making our house a home and so on.

We were working during the day and come back home and continue to finish off bits and pieces till late, hence "the night of the owls." Your dad was very funny, you know (she smiled). He was a charmer, respected life and absolutely adored humanity, an absolute gentleman.

Your dad went down with flu on the morning of the big night. It started with a sneeze, and we thought it's his allergy/ hay fever playing up and will go away. We were wrong. This was not looking good at all. He started drooling (I have never seen his nose running like that) and his eyes were tearing profusely, and he started to sweat as well. He looked terrible. I told myself, we are not going anywhere tonight.

"Let's get you to the doctor my love," I told him.

Never heard anyone referred to the doctor for floods, he joked as usual. One thing you don't know about him, he was very stubborn. If Nathan put his mind to something he never let go. He believed to change on the last minute brings about bad luck and he believed we do not deserve bad luck. He insisted I should go ahead without him and enjoy the night. I begged to stay but he would not let me.

He declined to go to hospital or to seek medical help and said he will take the remedy and will be ok and by the time I return he will be fit and running (she sobbed but trying to be strong at the same time).

He did not tell me that he had a surprise for me. Our best friends from college years were coming to town and booked at the same hotel. They were a nice couple and just by chance we were going to be together, sort of a re-union.

Chapter 3
The Shrink

No one is perfect. The Xhosa clan thinking tanks would say "Inxeba lendoda alihlekwa." This simple means thou shall not laugh at other people's misfortunes. Nikita used to take a micky of people visiting the shrinks. They will turn you into a zombie, she used to torment them. "Go in there and come back to me, I will prove it to you," she used to say. I will give a quick test to see if you are still fit. That was the test that was designed to make you doubt your decision to visit the shrink and/or even to doubt your sanity. Test yourself:

You smile – irrational.

You laugh loudly –you are deluded.

You become angry = Challenging behaviour.

You keep quiet or ignore her = you seem depressed.

You stand up and question her = you are very talkative/verbally challenging.

For the first time in her, life she pressed that button and made that appointment requesting to see the "shrink." Weird inn' it? For a shrink critic to request help from a shrink.

She definitely did not want this to be a public knowledge, fearing the backlash from her colleagues and others she humiliated big time. She was determined to make sure that whatever it takes her visit must be treated strictly confidential. She might have had a dig on the "shrink's code of ethics."

Nikita was a natural, she knew how to play games and she was good at that. She was a good researcher and very tactically natured.

Going to a shrink for the first can be daunting. Some of us have done it in our lives. We wonder what they will see, maybe stuff we were afraid to cough out.

This was not far from the truth as Nikita felt exactly the same. She needed help but was not prepared to open up. She was sitting on the branch of the fallen tree not far from their offices occupied about her forthcoming appointment. She was in deep thoughts, perhaps wondering about her career—how will this affect her progress (is it going to hinder it), her dignity, is she going to be stigmatised by this, and so forth.

Why don't I have confidence to face this shrink once and for all, she asked herself. That is why they boast that they are confidence builders. No, they are not, she was still fighting her inner thoughts, by the time you go there you have minus confidence and by the time you left them you have at least zero and you start all over again to build it up. They may adjust it at least to zero because of their digging and their reassurances. When you are genuinely troubled, every reassuring word is a blessing.

She saw her colleagues going in and out like buying candies and thought that's exactly what she was going to do. She was in for a shock as she was the beginner/ unknown to the services. There was a lot of administrative information need from her before she states her case. That drove her very potty. She was not aware that there is a string of other issues that needed to be ironed out. Her patience was eaten by Juice a long time ago (Juice is my youngest son Sisipho's dog). There is a saying that if your patience were eaten by a dog, you have none left. She should have known a shrink is not a fortune teller.

Chapter 4
Family Break

Like all mums do, Nikki's mum noticed the strain in her children. There was quite a social distance between the girls. The little one tended to be more quiet than usual. She could not bear the fact that Nikki is not her biological sister. Not that they did not like each other but, but this was the fresh wound and it really needed time to heal and quickly, but things were evaporating at the moment.

Nikki was rather uncontrollable. With the wake of the diagnosis of auditory hallucinations, this was proving to be difficult for her to cope and even more difficult to manage. The caring heart of the mum was bigger than that, there was nothing that could stand on the way of the welfare, unity and the happiness of her daughters.

When she mentioned a break to them, that came as a laugh to Nikki. She busted into a laugh, "a holiday, what a timing," she said.

"Give her a break, will you?" Intervened the young one.

"Of course, you quite right, she needs a break, let her go on holiday. It has been long due, you too can go as well, maybe you have some catching up to do."

"Shut up all of you, we are all going on holiday and that's final. We are family and we will stick as one. We are all going to be involved in the planning of this break and we are all going to enjoy it."

"Do not be so sure about that," said big mouth Nikita. Taking into consideration the recent crack into her health her mother decided to let that go but making sure that the holiday plan is on everyone's cards.

There was a half-smile of approval from Nikki's sister as if she was saying "yes we are back."

"Let us sleep on it today and tomorrow we will come up with ideas where we want to go and how are we planning to spend this time, right girls?" Mum concluded.

"Can I come and sleep with you?" The little girl asked.

"What's the excitement, did you wet your bed," replied Nikki jokingly and off they went arm in arm. Their mum did not know whether to cry, smile but relief was hidden all over her. Good night girls, she was breathing very heavily as she popped out those words and rushed to her bedroom and the floods of tears went down her cheeks, most probably of relief than grief at this time.

Nikki's mum barely slept that night due to excitement and the noise the girls made that night. She woke up very early as usual, prepared breakfast for her family and prepared herself for the holiday shops. Book it online, echoed the voice from the other room.

They knew it was not going to happen. Their mum was from the old school, she wanted to talk to someone face to face. Off went the big girl to the high street to book the holiday that she thought would bring her family together. It was more of a psychological reunion than anything else. The girls have given her the final decision about where to go and they were thinking local. She thought abroad as they have not been on holiday since her husband passed away.

The Caribbean, she thought and the Caribbean it was. That news was such a delight to the whole family. The screams of joy and the jumping up and down the bed told the story. They were overjoyed. They had only three days to prepare for the dream break, which was more than enough for them. Face book, tweets, text messaging, calls, you name it the girls were on it, that's today's children for you—social media crazy.

The Caribbean

It was the experience of their lifetime. They enjoyed every bit, the tour, the food, the beaches, they have been everywhere. They had absolute fun but sadly had to cut the holiday short as Nikki's mental health issues were taking its toll. The voices were in control again and were driving her crazy. All you could hear her say was shut up, please shut up. Nikita's mum did not foresee this.

"I thought these devils are gone," she said with a very angry disgusted voice.

"I wish they go forever from Nikki," added the little girl, hugging her mum.

"We need to go and find the doctor for Nikki," said her mum.

"No shrinks, no doctors please, I will be alright," said Nikki emphatically. But darling. No mum please, she cut her short.

It did not take long, and she was up on her feet again asking for a drink of water. "Oh, I hate this," she said. "It drives me potty. I am afraid we've got to go home. At least we have enjoyed most part of our break, it's only a couple of days left but I do not want to take any chances." The atmosphere was very dull, but they kept their spirits up to cheer Nikki who was pleading with them to stay up until the last day of their holiday.

The only way was home.

Chapter 5
The Twist

I don't want ever to see him in my life, she kept on saying those words repeatedly to her mum when talking about the Colonel—who she always referred to, as That Man. Although her mum did not say anything, you could see from her reaction that the feeling was mutual.

The tune suddenly changed from "doh," "reh" to so "me, reh." Was it the change of heart? Or the investment has reached its maturity. She was a blank slate. She was not playing her cards close to her chest, her cards were hidden under her bra (not that I am an expert in those things, but I have an inkling, it was a red bra).

Whatever she was thinking or planning she was in no mood for any unnecessary distractions. She was a lady in the move. She was interested into knowing who really the Colonel is.

Nikita was very relaxed, I should say, blank faced, emotionless with a childish, silly smile. She was in no rush but determined to design a good profile of this mysterious man (her so called biological father) who turned her life upside down. The Voices Have Spoken…

Her mum did not want to spoil the party. She had some reservations though. She did not think that was a good idea having seen how devastated she was on hearing that news. She was in sixes and sevens because she did not want this man in her path again. This was more difficult for her than it is for Nikita, but she decided to zip her food passage.

Let me admire the beauty of my daughter, at least she recovered from that misery state she was months ago. What will be, will be. She did as the mothers do, sacrifice for their children with all their hearts but her little angels had other ideas. She prayed, she cried but she knew that only God almighty will ease the pain and continued to pray for her daughter. She had no idea what Nikita's next move was.

The Voices Found Home...

Nikita wanted every detail about the Colonel. I did not know the man that much, he was your father's friend Nikki, she told her. That did not get her off the hook either. "My father surely told bits and pieces about him mum come on," she continued.

He has principles and is too particular about certain things.

"What things?" Nikki asked.

"He keeps his medication under the pillow, and he prepares his medication a week in advance, and he never missed even one tablet all his life. He goes fishing every Sunday afternoon because he believes is the blessed day for the fishes and God will give him some. No one enters his bedroom under any circumstances unless granted permission by him or his wife."

"Is his room always locked?" Nikki asked.

"I presume so, I do not know. That's a big house, are there cameras. He was a military man, what do you expect. But my father hated them. The difference was your father was a spy, so he had to dodge cameras all his life, that's why he hated them."

"Nikki, I cannot sit here all day talking about this man, I have work to do and I think you have more important things to do as well. Ok, that's enough for now."

"What do you mean for now, I am not discussing this anymore? Go away young woman."

They laughed and went separate ways. Nikki sat down and clutched her head and grimaced. Her mum did not notice that.

Chapter 6
The Distinction

"I have an invite," said Nikki rather very lukewarm. People invited at the so-called distinction receive it with such excitement because it is a once off especially if you are not from the military and not high up the ranks.

"What's that?" Her little sister asked.

"To be honest with you, I do not know. I have yet to find out and I have to find out very soon. Mum might know, maybe she and dad used to go. How did you get invited to something you do not even know? Let's go and get mum," she tried to avoid answering that.

"Where did you get that?" Her mum asked.

"Oh, you know this. We were coming to you to ask about it. This is my invitation. How did you get that?"

"I am Nikita, mum, remember that, the daughter of Lieutenant General Napego," she said twisting around.

"Now tell us, what is the distinction."

"Once asked about this he told people that this is about seasonal awareness. It is a celebration of the end and of the start of another season. It is only held once a year at the end of summer beginning of winter and vice-versa. It's his shows

I believe, and it is up to him when and how he wants to run them. Mostly military services are invited."

"And then what happens in the real thing?" They were becoming anxious, and the curiosity was mounting.

"It is quite a decent occasion. One of the chosen members of the round table becomes the master of the ceremony. He welcomes and addresses and also introduces the guest of honour. Like in the graduation ceremony. The guest of honour chooses what he wants to talk about, academic military things you know and other political staff.

"After that the guests mingle and meet and greet others, drinks served whilst they move around with the chosen band playing the music. There is a period, I think after the meal that people can sneak out to change if they want to disguise into a mask. This becomes fun as everything changes because you don't even recognise your partner unless you discussed it beforehand what you are going to wear and what type of mask will you be wearing. You dance with an absolute stranger. There will be short speeches in-between more to lift the spirits and have fun and some announcements of forth coming events but mostly it's just fun."

"How was dad?" Asked the little girl.

"That trickster. He tricked me into believing he was at the same primary school as I was when I was young, He knew almost everything I did, the name of my schoolteacher, my schoolmates where I used to take my breaks, the road I used to take home when my parents were not coming to take me from school etc. He knew my parents and my brother and my cousins. He asked me to guess who he was. I had no idea; I said all the boys' names I could remember and did not have a clue who he was. I kept on saying, your voice sounds familiar. He nearly fooled me."

"Did you not know what mask what he going to wear?"

"I guess he knew what he was going to do. We discussed the masks. I was going to be Barbie and he was going to be a wolf. So, I was comfortable because I know my husband was a wolf and he is not going to change the black tuxedo. He changed into a striped suit and was wearing mickey mouse. Can you believe that your dad wearing that? He was so funny. He was limping before we went. So, I was looking for my husband in black tuxedos, wearing a wolf mask and limping. In front of me was a mickey mouse, wearing a striped, black suit and dancing like a lunatic."

"How did you know it was him?"

"Come on put me out of this misery," I asked him. He knew I don't have patience and he whispered, "I am looking forward to that red wine tonight" and he half opened his mask and winked.

"You… (I nearly swore) …are in trouble mister, I promise you," I said. I was completely baffled.

Nikita was not very excited about the prospect of this distinction, seemed pre-occupied but was engaging with the conversation. No one bothered to ask. (Just in case the big V) Nikita was a blank book—there was absolutely nothing to read. She could smile whilst she is actually swearing at you and get her smile back.

The Big Day…

The window cleaner/ gardener did not finish his job the

previous day because of the thundering weather so he had to come back because the Colonel could not stand dirty, dusty and weeping windows as he called them.

Fortunately for him he finished almost everything except the back side of the building where no one could notice He was determined to make a good job of it though as he did not want to disappoint his master. He finished as quick as he could, left his workwear on the lawn and went for the shower at the back. Today he and his wife were invited (was very excited).

The street was a rainbow with different models of cars, ladies dressed to kill and the all blacks (all gentlemen were dressed in black tuxedos, white shirts and black bow-ties) It was a joyous sight, beautiful. The event was not open to the public, but the interest was immense.

The media came in numbers and the brass band in the garden was not disappointing either, they are always pleasing and energetic those boys, absolute entertainers. In contrast they were wearing all white, like angels they were. The atmosphere was so tempting to make you crash the party, but the decency of the occasion prevented that behaviour and brought about respect and admiration from a distance. That's what the rest of the people thought the word Distinction comes from.

It was quiet inside though, maybe people trying to organise themselves, some were fairly new to the occasion, trying to grasp the way forward shall I say climatise themselves.

The difference between this one and the previous ones was that they did away with that formality of the military uniforms and the medals (that really made other people very small) and went for the tuxedos instead. But that has not taken away the dignity of the occasion. At this stage the guests were unmasked, so that they can familiarise themselves with the surroundings and listen to the speeches from the dignitaries and to meet and greet old and new friends from all walks of life. Warm up drinks were served to break the ice.

By the time the gardener came back from the cold shower, Nikki had already thanked him in absentia for making her job much easier for leaving the window slightly ajar and the workwear to protect her dress.

She did her homework. She went in and out as if she lived in this place for some time. "Fuck…" she said quietly as she exited the Colonel's bedroom. The workwear was torn from behind. That seemed to bother her a little bit and within a whisker of a time she was inside dancing with others. She did not miss one bit.

The distinction was superb. They played games and everyone seemed to be enjoying every bit of them. It was a nice chaos, one journalist commented. As much as she was pre occupied Nikki seemed to enjoy a bit of that fun. She had to be more with it as they expected to hear from her about her day out. This is exactly what mum told us. You could have been the best man. The drink was rather taking the decision and she decided to call her mum to take her home She was a bit tipsy but trying to control herself.

They were so thrilled to see her in one piece.

"You are a distinction lady now," said her mum with a bit of controlled excitement.

"Oh, yes," replied Nikki throwing herself at the back seat. "It was fun, such, such fun. Where is my baby-sister?"

"She is waiting for you at home sweetheart."

"Why did you not bring her with you, mum?"

"She said she does not want to see the horrible man."

"She must not worry, that's she has a big sister, Nikita is going to clean this world for her. I am the saviour. I had these voices for the past three days now."

Her mum closed her eyes and quickly remembered she was on the wheel. She dreaded to hear that but thanks God she was safe and she could talk about them. "Were you alright out there?"

"Yeah, they were just talking and telling me what to do or shall I say commanding in a way, but I did what they wanted me to do but in my own way."

"Nikki you are clever," and she laughed.

These voices seem to be coming more often now, she thought whilst Nikki was repositioning herself on the chair. Are we there yet? Nearly there, sweetie. Ok, I am not sleeping. The little girl was up, and she heard the remote-controlled gate opening and she opened the door. Her mum parked in such a way that Nikki was not far from the entrance. They had trouble getting her in but she was ok. I am not drunk, I am alright, she reassured them. (Who was she kidding?).

I had fun, I met the dignitaries from here and abroad. They knew my dad and spoke highly of him which was satisfying. "I am proud of you," she said looking at his picture mounted on the wall. She was dropping off and her sister noticed that and thought shaking her head, no news tonight.

"Shall we help you to your bed and we can finish this tomorrow, the whole of it, not bits and pieces."

They agreed, Nikki feeling that the head is becoming heavier. They assisted her to her bedroom and straight to bed and it was lights out to all. Only their mum was left pondering, what kind of day did she have out there, having those voices.

Chapter 7
The Colonel

After the Distinction it was a bit quiet on the streets, but the news was still about the event. Although they do not all go there it is an important event for the community. Saturday's newspapers were full of it, radios and television were on it and the military boys were still boasting about it. It was as usual going to be the talk of the town for the next months to come. Not quite sure if it was a coincidence or a planned thing but usually there were no sporting events during that weekend.

Only the close family members were still in the premises as you can see from the distance trunks of cars opening and closing, a sign of packing of belongings. Everyone was getting ready to go. The big man liked solo Sundays as he wanted to reflect on things as he put it, there was a lot to reflect on indeed after that event. The big man was just standing and chatting to them, wishing them a safe journey home and thanking them for coming to the event and so forth. They were all in good spirits and certainly enjoyed the occasion, it did not disappoint, it was tops.

But from the family's point of view, you do not know until you get feedback from the audience. Off they went into a small convoy and guess what, you would not believe the cheering they got from the bystanders and people from the street. That was a signal of approval and thank you. The house from the outside was so pristine as if there was never an even full of hundreds of people, thanks to the community volunteers.

Sunday was no different either, paper boys were still ringing bell and the Sunday paper community were glued into those headlines as if it happened yesterday.

The Colonel was busy with his preparation for his fishing trip. He did not take long because all the equipment from the previous trip is packed in such a manner that they are ready for the next one, that's the Colonel for you. Within minutes he was set to go and off he went.

He perishes…

"Hey, hey, hey that boat is not manned," shouted the other fisherman.

"Which boat?"

"That one, that is the Colonel's boat."

"He is alright, he might be looking for something, he is a lone man that Colonel. He has been doing this for years now," replied the other.

"It is going all over man, it nearly capsized, I am telling you something isn't right with that boat."

"Ok, ok I am going to turn, you are a thorn in the nerve."

"No, no, no call the police, the ambulance whatever," shouted the fisherman, "Something has gone horribly wrong. Tell them it's Colonel Jones, he is face down on the boat, we don't know what happened, he is frothy in his mouth but looks as if he is still breathing but is not responding Oh God, please hurry, he does not look good at all. Colonel Jones, Colonel Jones," he continued to see if he can get a response.

Soon the beach was full of blue lights, helicopters etc. and he was airlifted to hospital. Colonel Gerald Jefferson Jones was pronounced dead on arrival to the hospital. The cause of his death was not known yet and was yet to be established.

In the dock…

News travel fast. The place was already full of people wanting to know what happened, shocked of the news about the Colonel, seeing his boat being towed to the deck. This was a very sad day to the community.

Hospital report…

The medics found that Colonel had a massive reaction to penicillin and had cardiac arrest. The rest of the information was handed over to the police as full investigations were about to start.

Chapter 8
The Behaviourist

The media was very busy as usual. That news was hot off the rail if not from the oven. Because of its pattern, it was becoming hot news and story to follow. It was on the headlines almost every day, in every major newspaper, radio stations, television and social media. This was the bread and butter of journalists and the talk of the town.

Seth, a final year human behaviour student at Temba Jackson Snowball College (aka TJS) seized the opportunity and decided to follow the story to enrich his studies. He was a loner, had few friends at the college and was not a social person. His hobby was scuba diving This was a moment for him to make a statement, so he thought. His friends used to tease him to swap the course for full-time forensics due to his curiosity in this mystery and other mystery murder cases. He started to put his foot where it does not belong—overstepping his natural curiosity.

His bedroom wall was full of newspaper headlines and posters about this story. His orchestration of events became suspicious and drew attention of the investigators. His interest caught the eye of the law. The police vowed not to leave any stones unturned, so behaviours like these were the main attraction given the fact that they drew a blank on their first attempt to crack the case. They were under extreme pressure and the Colonel was one of their own and the community was expecting some results and fast. Whoever tipped them must have seen or heard something very peculiar.

The bicycle city turned blue. The screeching of the tyres, the noise, the loudspeakers, children screaming not knowing where to go. This was scary, this was no talent show announcement, this was a "murder suspect" we were talking about.

"I lost count," commented the old man living around the corner. "I have never seen this since the war times when there's a suspected informant or a spy in the neighbourhood. This does not sound good at all. These boys mean business, this is not a social call."

"Come on inside, you don't know what will happen next granddad, this is not a movie," a middle-aged woman said.

"Looks more like it," mumbled granddad shuffling towards the door. "This is serious business, I can tell. Certainly not your own business, get in and shut the door behind you. If grandma was here, you would have a frying pan on your head by now. And you are still wandering why I had her assessed for a Zimmer-frame without wheels, the walking sticks proved too dangerous."

"For you or for her?" Asked his granddaughter.

"What do you think, I wanted to slow her down with those missiles?"

"Lock that door you two, I don't want any missiles in this house," intervened grandma unaware that this conversation was about her.

At the other end, the heat was on. "Seth Nkathazo, this is the metropolitan police, you are surrounded, get out of the house with your hands up," echoed the voice on the loudspeaker. There was silence. Seth never saw this coming. The mention of his name by the officer in charge shocked everybody. He was stoked, and so was everybody else who knew him.

The front door slowly opened, then silence, then the click of the machines and then silence again. The onlookers held their breaths.

What is he doing? The neighbours looked at each other in fear. The army of police officers advanced. You could see and feel the tension building. It was the churches united. Some were folding their arms with eyes closed, others were doing the sign of the cross, some had their hands clutched together between the chin and the forehead whilst some held their hands up high. The common denominator was the closure of the eyes.

This is really a small world and there is only one God. There was clearly more empathy than sympathy; one love, one heart as Bob Marley and Nqeberhu would have said in that situation.

A huge figure slowly came out the door with hands up. "Do not shoot, please do not shoot," he said with a shaky voice.

There were more advancing movements from the officers. They crouched like jungle wild cats but went past the "shaking leaf." Of course, they were not after him, they were looking for his tenant.

"This is your last chance, come out slowly with your hands up." There was no doubt in that voice, and you could sense that it was two-fold— "Surrender or my colleagues will get ready to get you dead or alive."

The other officials were questioning the landlord to find out what was going on inside there. He was not off the hook as well.

Bang, bang, a loud sound of gunfire came from the direction of the house. "Shots fired, shots fired," shouted the other officer.

"Hold your fire, hold your fire," shouted the officer on the loudspeaker. There was silence, but the tension was growing. Everyone took cover. It was not clear whether that was coming inside the house, outside or on top of the roofs as it was "raining" guns.

Seth came out at last amazed with how many officers have paid him a visit. He waived the white cloth in his left hand and slowly followed the commands. He got down to his knees as the officers rushed to handcuff him, reading him his rights and leading him to the police van.

The police in attendance took the "white cloth" with a frown. This is his underpants, he told his colleague—he clearly does not know when to take this thing off, does he (they secretly laughed it off).

News travel fast. The staff and other students at the college could not believe what they heard and/or seen. The campus temporarily became the home of investigatory/intelligence team and the media. The story was bigger than anyone could imagine. This was no ordinary crime, the world classed this as a very serious offence. This was planned, carefully orchestrated murder. Whoever did this, knew exactly what he/she was doing. It was not clear at this time whether the perpetrator was working on his/her own, had an accomplice or working as a group. Time will tell.

Not to let his intentions known to his fellow colleagues and the college authorities nearly let him drown in his own soup. That's the price you pay in society when you behave in a suspicious way.

Chapter 9
The Behaviourist Questioned

It was the biggest shock at the college as everyone knew Seth as the bright quiet man, but some had their reservations, calling him the dark horse and some calling him weird beast of the west. Students and college authorities had divided opinions about this whole incident.

Everyone was surprised by this. Seth had no idea what was coming his way as he was only thinking he was doing the best for his career. He had no doubt he was innocent but was very shaken by the developments.

There was too much attention in this case as the victim was of high profile. On the day of the arrest Seth was taken in the investigation room but they had to wait as rightly so he would not open his mouth unless he had a lawyer beside him. He had already told them he knew nothing about this, he was just interested in the case as everybody else and he never met the man in person only saw his pictures on the newspapers. "That is all I am going to say, I want my lawyer now," he said. He was trying to be bold but deep down, he was scared.

This gave them an opportunity as well to tie the loose ends Seth did not realise the magnitude of what he has let himself in by his curiosity up until the interrogation process. Is this really happening must have been what is on his mind now. You have done nothing, you have done absolutely nothing, he quietly reassured himself, trembling with fear because he knew of the cases, he read himself that people do go to prison for crimes they did not commit. That thought on its own scared him to death. Where is this lawyer? He kept looking at the door, it was dark there was no hope.

A tall dark figure appeared through the door. Before she was even introduced by the officer who brought her, Seth was already on her arms tearful and thanking her for coming and pleading her to get him out of that place. "Ok have a seat," she said to him.

"What have you done to him; she asked the officer?"

"Absolutely nothing," replied the policeman.

"Can I a few minutes with my client please?" She asked the officer.

"Certainly," he said, and he stepped outside.

"I did not have a chance to introduce myself, I am Selin Ob from the legal aid, I will be representing you in this case. I want you to calm down, relax and tell me exactly what happened here," she said to Seth.

"Nothing so far," he said, "I told them I do not know anything about this, I was just curious in the case for my career," he continued.

"Did you, do it? Sorry I am a straightforward person and I like honesty. No, no not at all."

"Thanks, let's go and sit down."

The officer joined them on the table.

"My client had nothing to do with this, does not even know the victim. He is a student for God's sake and is entitled to have posters for study purposes. We are going home."

Before he opened his mouth, there was a knock on the door calling him, "Release him, his alibi is watertight" was the message.

He stepped inside with a wry smile on his face, you are free to go Mr Nkathazo, thanks for your time both of you.

Thank you, they both welcomed the decision and off they went, smiles all over Seth's face, thanking his lawyer. It was back to the drawing board for the boys in blue This put more pressure on the police department.

Chapter 10
The Mystery

No one wanted to be engaged in any kind of speculations at this moment. This was not an ordinary simple case. If the Colonel was allergic to penicillin, did he not know that and if he knew that why did he take it? If he did not take it himself who gave it to him? This was the chief investigator's headache for now. The first point of investigation was the dock (so they thought).

The security at the dock was clear that when the Colonel came in, he was alone as usual in the same fishing mood, always smiling and cheerful. I even asked him if he read the paper about the Distinction and laughed and told me that he is going to see me there, next season. There was absolutely nothing wrong at all. The attendant at the deck echoed the same. He helped him untie his boat, same old Colonel, never changes, spoke about the weather, how nice it was and asked me about my family, very good man.

The Colonel was seen alive by the other fisherman when he caught what could be called the catch of the day, a big one when he shouted with joy as fisherman do, up until he was found unresponsive by the other two who called for help.

The area of investigation was widening from family members who were with him during the weekend to the crowds of people who attended the Distinction and beyond. This was the worst nightmare. They had to take the guest list and interview every possible suspect including the dignitaries who were there. This was by far not the easiest task. The forensic team had already been to the boat and the house. They found blood but it matched the Colonel's DNA and now had to ascertain if it is his blood, but they were waiting for the results from their senior personnel.

The blood found in Colonel's bedroom was not his, as had no evidence of blood loss. This was proving to be more difficult than it was anticipated. The public was spared the agony as the focus was on the close family members now. They had to be careful because they did not want to leave the family of a very respected man torn apart unnecessarily. They had to ensure their interviews are tactful, dignified and fact finding not accusing and or assuming.

The only closest relatives were his daughter and his younger brother. The daughter was ruled out because she did not even go near the house as she was sick with flu and did not want to come and give it to everybody. She was due to see her father after the fishing trip for dinner. That left only one suspect, the younger brother who in the past did not see eye to eye with the Colonel according to the family information. He was a practicing Pharmacist, but the business was not going well. He was helped once by the Colonel, but he blew it. There were reasons to ask him some questions as his DNA matched the one found in the Colonel's room.

He denied having anything to do with his brother's death and he offered to undergo a lie detector test and he passed it.

He claimed they were always together and at no point was he left alone in his room, and he had no clue what his brother was taking medication wise. He knew he was allergic to penicillin from their childhood. He cooperated in every aspect of the investigation and offered to help if needed and was released without a charge. The department was left with no suspects nor witnesses, and they were under such tremendous pressure.

Were they quick into releasing the guests who attended the Distinction? They were criticised by the public because there could have been some key witnesses there.

Chapter 11
The Chase Is on...Catch Me If You Can

Let the games begin…

How it surfaced was not the chief's concern at this point nor in the latter stages either, he had a murder case to solve. Nikki fitted the description of the girl they saw on CCTV footage in the Colonel's house and possibly the rumours that she might be the Colonel's daughter can answer the DNA mystery. A visit to Lt General Napego's residence was a must.

This was becoming more complicated or rather more complex and confusing. This puzzle needs to be solved and solved quickly, he told himself He knew that was not going to be as easy as ABC because Nikita was a very smart and manipulative girl. She took too much from the General. I am not going to create. any waves, I am going there myself, it is going to be an official visit, but I will attend to it solo, for now. I never met this lady in person, she was very young when I visited her dad, look how fast time goes, here am I now coming to investigate her for murder. Such is life.

He parked his car in such a way he could see all the exits of the house, just in case there is a runner. As soon as Nikki's mum saw the chief, she thought of Nikki and the voices and she did not think of any reason why the chief of the police can pay her a visit. The hard knock on the door confirmed the visit.

Account from Nikki's mum…

She was scared and confused. She did not know whether to appreciate the visit or not but decided it will be rude not to as she respected the chief and had not seen him since her husband died and they were very good colleagues. She gave the chief a very warm welcome and the and gave her a big hug. They said down and before the chief said anything, she asked the chief if this is about Nikita.

"Why are you asking that?" The chief asked.

"You know children, Chief, the older they are the more they become a worry. She has not been herself lately. I think her mental health issues are climbing up a bit. These voices are troubling her, and they come so very often now. They drive her crazy and this is worrying me because when they are there, she becomes no longer my little Nikki. They turn her into an animal I do not know." She tried to hold tears back. "Oh Chief, sorry to bother you with my problems. What do I owe this honourable visit to?"

She made it easier for him to open the subject with Nikita but made it difficult at the end because the chief has to open another painful wound for the parent now.

"In what way do those voices turn her into an animal?" He wanted to dig more about Nikki's behaviour lately before he gets into my main reason for his visit.

"I would not say she becomes violent, no, Nikki is a smart girl."

"She is the James Bond of the house," her little sister said.

"I disagree because she hates blood. I cannot describe her, but all I know, she will make you pay."

The little girl came with hot drinks and biscuits. They had coffee and tea whilst the chief was preparing his lines.

"Sorry to hear about her mental health issues. I hope she pulls through; she seems like a strong girl. Did she seek any help with those voices?"

"Yes Chief, I think she was seeing one of the psychiatrists in town, Dr Pentz."

"Where is she now?" The chief asked.

"To be honest with you, Chief, I do not know. The last time I saw her was shortly after the Distinction. She said she wanted some fresh air and will visit her friend."

"Oh, did she go to the Distinction?" The chief asked.

"Yeah, she was invited, by who and how, do not ask me. She would not tell us. Did she finally tell you who invited her?" She asked the little girl.

"No mum, same answer she gave you, I am the daughter of Lt General Napego."

"She learnt a lot from the General yeah, not much to give," added the chief.

"More than I did, it's like they were partners at work or partners in crime, Chief."

"Talking about crime, this is the reason why I am here. I am not going to beat about the bush. Your daughter is a suspect in the murder of Colonel Jones."

"No way Chief, she was here with us the whole day on Sunday, she never went anywhere day and night. We even went to church all of us and went out for the Chinese, I swear to God."

"I am afraid it is more complicated than that Mrs Napego. We need to question your daughter about this and the sooner she turns herself in for questioning the better."

"How did she know the Colonel?" The chief continued.

"I do not think she knew the Colonel that much, maybe from the news or media, because the Colonel was not our favourite topic in this house, as you may know."

"Enlighten me please, there is a lot I do not know in this town."

"Colonel is Nikita's biological father, Chief."

"Can I have a glass of cold water please?" The chief asked. He was looking at breaking the things one by one. More vital information was being thrown into his bag and his visit could prove crucial for this case. He did not want to rush her as he knew if she wants to refuse answering she has every right, she is not a suspect here.

"How did she take it, given the fact that she was very good buddies with your husband?" He asked.

"Not very well. This was heart breaking. Not that I was worried about how they would get on, that was not my concern. My main worry was how it will affect her and her sister, and how things will be for all of us, now that my husband is gone because he was the one hell of a guy, support, comfort, love, you name it you get it. He knew how to deal with any situation in life."

"I know, that's why he was not just a general but a lieutenant," added the chief trying to soothe the situation.

"They do not have to know each other. I am here and I am his father and that's final. Those were my husband's words when we received the news. So, they did not know each other? No one wanted to know about it, if you know what I mean, on one. Oh, I feel like screaming very loud. She only knew last year when we needed a donor for her sister. She offered.

"Stupid me I could have stopped her but it was one of those things. They were not compatible, and she kept on asking questions. I had to tell her. I was distraught. I felt dirty, guilty and ashamed as if it happened yesterday. That Colonel raped me, whilst his friend, my dear husband (who had no idea what was going on) was waiting for me at home. How cruel, she sobbed. My husband trusted him as a colleague and a friend."

"I know, I know they were close friends," said the chief.

"Nikki cornered me with a lot of questions and hardly could answer. She seemed very disappointed, but this was no cause for concern. My concern was how she quickly accepted it and told me let's lay it to rest mum. She apologised for her behaviour and understood that this was not my fault as she spoke as a grown woman really and supported me. My behaviour just came at the heat of the moment, it did not have any meaning, I love, I always did, and I always will. Those words were convincing, and I knew they were coming straight from her heart, I believed her."

A telephone rang. They were all ears. The little girl answered the phone. She was barely few minutes, not uttering any words only, "umm, yep, umm, and finally said no, I am not in the mood to go anywhere today, and my mum has a visitor, the chief of police. Maybe tomorrow. Thanks. Bye."

"Who was that?" Her mum asked.

"My friend, she wants to go out to the park."

"Thanks for your time, Mrs Napego, you have been of good help. Do not forget to tell Nikki about my visit and my advice. Hope she gets well with those things, you know." (referring to the voices)

"Thanks very much chief, news are not good, but thanks for visiting and thanks for letting me know."

These children have learnt a lot from their father—the General. I bet that was from Nikita (referring to the telephone call that came whilst he was there). They are definitely going to be playing games with us. He knew they were up against a steep hill because it was the early stages and they have yet to question, not even to trial a suspect from this case and the society is waiting anxiously to hear the words "arrested." This suspect does not look an easy nut to crack.

It was back to the drawing board for the chief. At least this time with something in hand. He knew one or two things about her suspect, and he dared not to under-estimate her.

He has learnt a lot from the general so he was expecting this not to be an easy case. He was determined to get results though. He did not want to rush and go and brief her team first before tying all the loose ends. His next move was to go and visit Dr Pentz downtown. He wanted to be sure and be prepared with what they were going to deal with, in terms of behaviour, mood swings, danger and general behaviour.

Chapter 12
It Is a Matter of
National Security

The lockdown...

Were they on target, or was it just one of their well-known near misses? This was a bizarre command from the police department. That does not happen very often in hospitals or am I out of this world.

It was a very busy morning in Johnson Memorial Hospital, the Super Wednesday, as they used to call it, where the interns have to prove their worth. You would hear a feather thumping on the floor on that day. Professor Dove was allergic to the noise, manmade noise. He hated those clapping high heeled shoes, who does not? Are they fashionable these days, anyway? He never personally said it and never confronted or told off anyone but do not quote me on this.

I heard through the grapevine that one of the consultants came into one of his monthly meetings wearing one of those clapping high heeled shoes and he did not matter a word and if I can put it in one of the native South African languages called is Xhosa, "Wamthi baxu, wamqala ezinyaweni wamnyuka." In this context it means that he gave her a telling look. (He starred at her from toes to the head).

Since then, everyone wore smart, formal and flat or floor friendly high heeled shoes (no clapping allowed ladies, please). The relatives never miss this event, it was dubbed "the quiet war of the brains," the clash of the moon and the sun (some might say). The atmosphere was so tense, a very windy or stormy situation for the faint-hearted and shallow-minded.

As an intern, its either you come fully prepared for the onslaught, know your patients from A to Z—their diagnosis, aetiology, treatment (indication and contra-indication) and always have plan B just in case there are unwanted complications (as if there are wanted complications) or stay at home and avoid humiliation. The battle of the bold and the beautiful. Medicine practices does not want weaklings (who does in this challenging world?).

The new recruit, I wonder how she knew Professor Dove's likes and dislikes, preferences or even about the event itself on this day etc. Tucked on her shoulder was a turquoise clutch bag bouncing nicely on her red three-piece suit, trousers slightly sweeping the floor, red painted toenails floating in her turquoise pencil heeled shoes. Very elegant, I must admit.

She was all smiles, had a very pleasant attitude and noting everything that was said on the presentation by the team. She was active and seemed to ask relevant questions to the annoyance of the new interns. She was cleverly avoiding attention because she knew the pressure is on the interns and by having an input on the early stages the honours will be on the interns to grab the ball and keep it in their court. She did not have to prove anything. You certainly do not want a stream of questions when you are hot under the collar. This behaviour put pressure and that urge to produce something fruitful on the interns.

Ideas flew from left to the right. Who does not want a good report or recommendation from Prof. Dove? Every intern wants to get noticed. Professor never miss that good question, "What do you think?"

Every participating guest or student know that readiness is the key because he threw that question around the room irrespective of who you are. This kind of question is a pressure relief and gives you time to think about things. It does not expose you but makes you cute and above all you do not lose track of what you were doing nor concentration.

It was time for young professionals to put the theory into practice.

Everyone was drawn to the process and did not want to miss out on the experts' comments and recommendations and the trick of the trade.

Suddenly, there was chaos, police swarmed the place and demanded the hospital authorities to close all exits and entrances to and from the hospital with immediate effect. That sort of urgency disrupted everything as there were no detailed explanations for the request or a demand except that "this is a matter of national security."

They are following a lead and the suspect has been seen entering the hospital. The place went into total scare as it was turned upside down by uniformed police and their allies. They ransacked the place, there were police everywhere, on the roof, in the basement, every department as if they are waging war.

They were looking for the lady in red. The new recruit was dressed for the occasion, red suit a white coat and a black stethoscope around her neck, very professional indeed.

Meanwhile…

Earlier in the morning Dr Zukza decided to do his rounds before his regular schedule to avoid clash with the big event. He reviewed most of his patients, referred some to relevant specialists and discharged some home. This was an unusual busy day, and everything was done so quick and to perfection as if that was the last day of the universe. All those who were discharged were out of the building before the chaos began, transport, transfer letters, follow up appointments all set.

Then…

After the rounds by Dr Zukza the new recruit came to the desk enquiring about Patient B claiming that she made an appointment with the patient prior to his discharge to visit him. But missed Dr Zukza because of the timing of the conference and the change of the times for the doctors' rounds. She is glad that he is discharged though and will follow up the discharge plan with Dr Zukza in due course.

She asked for the address of the next of kin and apologised for that and said she must have left her notebook in her work handbag, which is understandable, and she want to visit the next of kin straight after the conference. She was really convincing and there was nothing suspicious about her, she was genuine and seem to know the patient and Dr Zukza.

It was a busy day and did not want to keep the doctor waiting as she was going back to rejoin the conference. She was in no hurry or panic, she even offered to wait and come after the conference if we were busy, very understanding of the nature of work and pressures we are in. She was very nice.

I like her. She had an American accent. This was a bizarre day. I think it came at a right time no one seemed to be paying any attention.

The chief was not pleased at all by the development of events. When he was asking around the staff it seems no one has taken notice of this lady whilst she was doing things right up their noses. This is insane, he lashed out! You liked her, she had an American, tomorrow she will be speaking Zulu.

"What's that?" The nurse assistant asked.

"Cha, abe sekhuluma phela," answered the other one in Zulu and they looked at each other and laughed.

"Do you think this is funny?" he barked.

"No, sorry Sir you just reminded me of my native language, I am from KwaZulu-Natal in South Africa."

The chief assembled his crew and gave them orders to follow the lead to the patients next of kin's address which Nikita requested. The convoy followed suit. Nikita followed them cautiously in a blue Volkswagen Beetle Convertible with the top wide open.

Patient D's residence…

The ambulance crew could not revive him, he was found lying on the side of his bed, dead. Seemingly he was trying to reach for his nebulisers as he was gasping and struggling to breath.

More headache for the chief of police—

The patient was found uncomfortably dead in his own house after a visit by the suspect—were the headlines of the week.

Chapter 13
Void

"Void!" the desperate cry exploded.

Abort, abort! There sounded to be an urgent meaningful tone behind that voice. Whoever shouted that seemed to have high authority (if there is such a thing) because everyone stopped immediately as if he is controlling the whole world, there was calm, quietness and the traffic seemed to slow down, drivers behaving well and there were no raging bulls on the road.

Somewhere, somehow there seemed to be an emergency, blue lights everywhere, tyros screeching. They must be on the money, one would think. Whoever they were chasing was in big trouble, they came in numbers these boys and they meant business. They stopped and waited for the next command whilst some did the Lewis Hamilton's doughnuts and went back to their stations. I think they were tired of chasing ghosts and barking at the wrong trees.

The convoy filled the road their sirens deafening, accompanied by the helicopter this time thoroughly searching the area. Soon the small town turned blue with sounds of clicking of guns, big and small. Heavily armed was an understatement, they were really loaded. With the kind of artillery, they were carrying they meant business. They were at war. I did not envy the culprit.

Nikita was not far from the action, watching. She thought that was the perfect moment to switch seats with the law. She wanted to make them sweat, didn't she. Make a move now or never, the latter was not on the cards. Chase their tails, do not stay very close, not a sniff.

This is becoming a dangerous game. Where is the better place to hide or shall I say to take a breather other than where the chaser has been already. She looked left and then right and grinned as she reached for her mobile phone. She paused for a while, "Not with my personal phone," she muttered to herself. They might be on it by now, I think.

Why don't you just go before this hit national news with your pretty face around the globe. Taxi! No, no, these guys are the first point of enquiry especially in cases like these. They also think it's an honour to speak to the police especially when they are clean and moreover, they do not stand the heat. I do not want to make a scene. Walk to the nearest hotel or motel just in case there is a vacancy. Absolutely not, no walking, if spotted you will be a sitting duck, echoed the voice.

It won't be long now before they realise that they have got it the wrong and the search is still wide open. Think, think Nikita. Just do it! A command snapped. After all they will really be wasting taxpayers' money if they come back to search this town again.

A little boy passed by with a mobile phone in his back pocket. She stopped short of asking him to lend me his phone when she thought, that is too risky and to add more children have good memory or an adult might be following. Just when she was thinking about that, "slow down Justin," a tall, hefty bodybuilder-like giant appeared.

Oops, close call, she sighed with relief. Not that she was scared of him but the thought of him questioning her who she was, what did she want with his son or whatever their relationship was, would have wasting her time and invited lots of interest that was not desired at this moment. She would not allow him to dig on her. She was the person of interest in this situation, she must stay calm and collected. She did not want people to put two and two together. What a giveaway that would be. "Her job was not finished yet," she said, "A lady— NOPE," she continued, "they like to yep, yep, those gobblers. They do not need to be asked before they unknowingly blow the whistle, no wonder Football Association don't have many of them."

A middle-aged man came by. "A perfect fit," she said, "Shrug your shoulders, shake up your bra contents and their minds go to sleep. Believe me, the only senses working at this time at these weaklings are the sense of sight and the sense of hips (if you know what I mean) and they do not look at you, they screen you. Go for it! Nikki," she pumped herself up and went for him.

"Oh, hello. My phone has just died. I need to make an urgent call, can I borrow yours if you don't mind, it won't take long, please," she went on.

"Of course, love," replied the man. "Oh, let me not give you this one, it's my wife's precious phone, she may start to wonder whom I was calling to and start to interrogate me."

"Umm, too much information," she muttered to herself.

"Here, take this one. He gave her his new iPhone X. Tell me about bragging," she said silently trying not to push her luck. "Thank you very much, much appreciated. I will make sure I delete everything before your precious wife put her hands on it. I do not want to put you into trouble," she reassured him. She dialled, got through, erased the existence of the call, gave the phone back to him and thanked him. Can we… (She was gone before he even finished what he was about to say)

Down the police station the mood was not that bright, they have been taken for a ride again. The diversion worked perfectly for Nikita. They were falling into her traps. "We don't tell them to jump, we show them we are jumping move does work, thanks dad," she said smiling and looking to the skies. (Where the old man is resting).

"Damn, this girl is something else," said the chief banging his desk. It's time for us to up our game. The next of kin address she requested at the hospital and desperate to get to it was just a diversion. She did not need that address, she wanted us to go there so that she can finish her job (which she did). Questions were asked, how did she know about this man? This was an old case; how did she know about it? How did she know where he lives? It is not on the records as it was removed for security reasons long time ago. Is she working with someone? This is the second murder in our hands, and we have yet to find this suspect. This girl is a step ahead of us, I admit (he did not say that loud).

The community is running scared and losing faith in us. They are afraid as this is taking a serial killing pattern now. People were already questioning their fitness and capability to protect them. She might have not gone that far. Roadblocks were set around the town and the surrounding areas immediately. They were not sure if she was driving or not as no one saw her except in the hospital.

Chapter 14
I'll Be Damned!

It was business as usual for Tommy T. as he was known. People these days do not mind their own businesses. Everything that brings money home 'will do' legally or otherwise.

Tommy T. was running a very risky, unpopular business targeting the married, unfaithful rich people of all genders. His defines on this sordid business was, 'teaching cheaters a lesson.'

"I am not blackmailing them; I am trying to correct their behaviour. Of course, it comes at a price, nothing is free," claimed Tommy T. "There is a lot of research involved and had to finance my work and pay for my equipment and my associates," he would add sarcastically. He knows he was playing with fire as he had ducked few bullets before and has ben braved to continue his acts (dirty money is infectious), as some victims proved to go lengths into protecting their marriages.

Tommy T. liked people who gossiped a lot and would pay healthy figures for a vital information including names, venues, addresses and times of alleged sins. He liked the religious sinners. He was fast becoming a known figure as some housewives will hire him if they suspect a foul from their partners. He was good in digging information and he was discreet, and he kept his promise. His business was booming, or shall I say his bank balance was healthy and his bank statement was not only ending on the first page.

He expanded his business and recruited researchers who really were up to the game and had their ear on the ground and had six eyes (front, sides and back). He was becoming greedy now and had regulars and introduced an agreement clause, 'You pay me, and I will keep my mouth shut clause.'

Nikita thanked her lucky stars that she did not bump into Tommy T. whilst busy on her own mission. She managed to avoid Tommy T's cameras which was right on her nose as thought about it, still shaking. I'll be damned, she exclaimed with a big sigh of relief. She heard about this man but whatever he did not concern her, up to this night. This has to stop, she told herself silently and the more she thinks about it the more this was troubling her.

I must stop this before it came to stage when it really haunts me and put me into deep un-reversible trouble. What if she caught me on his camera? This would defeat my purpose isn't. That would have been a pay-rise for Tommy T. and game over for me. This is game changer, sorry Tommy T. What is he doing here? It is a good thing that his operation concentrated on the guy next door because if he was where I am now that could have been disastrous. What was he doing on the roof anyway? To think of it that could have been a nasty clash and more disastrous for me.

That would have instantly made me a person of interest. I swear I will never let your cameras ruin my operations. I need to clear this area soon and fast and I cannot do that with cameras hanging around me. Tommy T. must lay off for a bit, and that is not a negotiable request.

To think of it, this was really a very close call. It was a good thing I backed off. By the time I come back there will be less scrutiny and there will be plenty of time to settle my scores. I must end this.

It was one of those English shivering nights, a day after the devastating Storm Eunice wrecked North Wales, Scotland and North and East of England. That was an unforgettable windy Friday in February for some whilst others just wanted to forget about it and wash the blues away. People were warned not to travel unless it was necessary to do so. Some ignored the warnings and even ignored the Covid 19 Pandemic restrictions. Risking penalties. Nikita pondered whilst drafting her next plans to temporarily cut off Tommy T.

She needed space and did not want any interruptions. She did her homework and found that Toomy T. chills at Cross Bar on Sundays an hour before his crew joins him probably to discuss plans for the following week and give feedback of the previous week ending (whatever). This man thinks this a legal operation. She went straight and sat on the corner table pretending to be a regular waiting for her accomplice. Nikita was waiting for her moment to pounce.

It was not that long, and the eagle landed. Tommy T. whispered to the barman and went straight to the Gents. Oh! How did he know I don't have enough time for this nonsense? One glance at the crowd, Nikita figured no one was interested to go to the loo, it was rather too early for them to go. She went straight to the Ladies. Both entrances were covered by CCTV cameras except inside.

By the time Tommy T. was gearing to flush his product down the toilet, a help was in hand, someone else did the job for him.

"Do not move an inch." That was a command not to be repeated as he felt a cold barrel shaping his ear. He did not need any explanations; he knew exactly what that clicking sound meant.

"Now, listen carefully. I am not going to repeat what I am going to say to you now. Your next move is to go back to your table quietly. Do not go to the barman, your drinks will be served. Do not use or answer your mobile phone, your crew knows exactly where you are. There is a notice on your table saying Do Not Disturb, and there is a notebook. So, you are going to get busy and draft your next move with your crew. Your table is Number 9.

"When you wake up, I want you to address your crew that due to circumstances beyond your control, the operation is suspended until further notice. No questions asked and no explanations given." Currently, the revolver was nearly piercing his big elephant ears.

"I know you are waiting for them as I speak. This must happen with immediate effect. Do you understand me? I do not want your answer, just shut up and listen. Consider this your very, very lucky day.

"You are going to do exactly what we have discussed here word by word. Do I make myself very clear?" She nearly burst his eardrum.

Before he even whispers yes, a cold pounding iron turned his lights off.

Chapter 15
DIY

A white coat and a stethoscope around the neck means a doctor. There is no question about that and nothing suspicious about that either. It is good enough to attract the community's curiosity and can easily divert their attention as well. They always can afford posh cars these doctors, of course to maintain their status, their celebrity style of living, not the Detective Colombo style. Routine call visits for check-ups in the evenings are more common for family doctors especially after their clinics.

It was one of those cold January evenings, drizzling steadily clouding the visibility. A black Mercedes Benz convertible just slowly parked in front of MK's residence. MK was a well-known celebrity photographer who made his name and fortune with well-known politicians, head of states, film directors and producers and to a greater extent the global actors. He was a well-known figure and people in all walks of life were in and out of his studios.

The street was dubbed Posh Street because of its reputation or visitation if you like with very expensive performance posh cars.

That must have been why his appointment was around this time, figured the onlookers. This guy has a very busy schedule.

She went in (the doctor) and stayed for a little bit longer—typical medic might be checking him over, taking bloods. "You know these doctors," said the neighbour. We did not see her leave. He usually accompanies his visitors to their cars when they leave probably to say goodbye but he never to this medic, I don't blame him, who loves doctors with needles and dentists with hammers, pliers and screwdrivers.

After a lengthy consultation, the doctor decided it was time to finish her duties, time to go and so she went.

Behind the scenes...

Nikita went in swiftly into the living room. This was just a standard procedure in MK's residence, go straight in and drinks will be served before you state your case—charming yeah. She patiently sat there waiting to be attended to. "Hello, can I help?" The boss emerged from the bathroom gold sliding doors.

"I was about to retire to bed, you are lucky to get my attention," he continued.

"Thanks for that," she replied. He had no idea who he was speaking to. "Just finished my evening duties," she added.

A bottle of wine came around, courtesy of MK. He moved around the settee and brought two silver crafted wine glasses. Nikita was fuming inside but trying to keep her cool. "Is it really what is happening here?" She asked herself looking across the room. She thought about disturbing stories behind MK's residence and tried successfully to control the tears running her cheeks. Is this what being famous is all about? Is this the high price we pay for being poor? What does he think the purpose of my visit is? I do not drink white wine, thank you.

She said trying to buy some time to ready herself. He did not know what was in store for him. She did not stop smiling. He might have been thinking, "this is the luckiest day for me." At the other end, "now this is your chance," the voices continued their stance on Nikita's head. Hoping no one will come at this stage and no one is around the house, she asked for a tour of the residency. Then came a bottle of vintage red wine and his smile seemed to widen.

"I do not want your dirty wine, I want to cleanse your blood you dirty monster," she muttered to herself.

"Are you saying something?" He asked.

"No, I am just flattered," she forced a smile. She clutched her handbag and stood up waiting to be directed. Off went the leading hand—she continued to clutch her bag firmly as if to tell him nicely she was not holding anyone's hand. The message was crystal clear, but the devil was still rejoicing because he never knew what the word NO means (even in capital letters).

Interestingly the tour started with the bedroom, why not the studio because it is the most prominent business feature of this building. That is the reason why people come here in the first place. I am on borrowed time; I am in the mood (the reverse of what you think). You are wasting time Nikita, a command echoed. Be calm Nikki, be calm, she told herself. Do not worry, you have a whole bottle of wine to dice with, she reassured herself. Do not raise any suspicion, she continued. Bad, bad man, the voice kept on, putting more pressure on her.

She kept on smiling and appreciating the tour. She looked cool but really hot under the collar. She heard so many stories about this place and she wanted to figure out, satisfy her curiosity and do what she thought was necessary. She wanted to take things one step at a time. You are going to lead the way to your destiny mister, she smiled and look at the pine decorated ceiling, "umm, great art," she commented loudly.

"You like it," he smiled, looking very proud.

"Very much so, it's a nice piece of art, that must have cost a fortune," she was wondering where and when this tour is going to end.

"You could not even guess how much that cost me my darling," he said, impressed and not really minding his distance Nikita could feel his heartbeat. She did not react. She wanted this party over, nice smooth and without struggle.

I hate warm wine; she told him not hiding her glance on her wristwatch. The studio was like a mini town decorated for Christmas. It was huge and really impressive. Wow, she could not close her mouth and by doing that she opened the flood gates. He was easing up; she was becoming more tense. "Take it easy, we have not formally introduced ourselves yet."

"Oh, you quite right, how silly of me," he said looking full of himself.

"I'll be damned!" Whatever she saw made her very angry but tried to control herself. "Are you a medic?" She asked inquisitively. He giggled but could not give a straight answer to the question. Nikita was boiling inside. He finally led her to what she suspected has been the "normal routine" if you like, for unsuspecting visitors or guests. Wine and dine, more wine than dining and a large dose of un-prescribed drugs.

"I don't play games," Nikita tried to set the record straight. He did not get the message.

He opened the bottle and poured the wine for her and for him. He took a sip and lit his cigar and offered her one. He looked pleased. "These are no local brands baby," he bragged. She hated cigars but did not refuse the offer.

"Where are they from?" Nikki asked as if to say, I have enough of this nonsense. He continued to drink as if he was going to miss the next train. He looked anxious but playing cool. Nikita was no dummy. "Oh, where is the bathroom, this wine is taking its toll now." He did not notice even it was never touched.

She nicked out and he sneaked something into her drink. Nikki expected that, seeing from his reactions and his history. She kept him busy.

Nikita asked if she could propose a toast. "Yes, sure why not," he said with a wide smile. Hope was written all over his face. "Oops, to what?" Nikki asked.

"Anything my love, anything you are in charge." He was really looking turned on to life exchanges, she crossed their hands exchanging wine glasses and suddenly changed her mind. And told him, "Not yet—you are not having mine."

"You're in such a hurry darling? Aren't you?"

"No, no, not, at all," he answered, sounding anxious but looking forward to the surprise.

"I hope I am not holding your work or maybe you are expecting a bunch of children coming with their mum with a full bucket of washing, singing daddy, daddy we are home."

"Oh, she is very funny too," he laughed.

It takes one lousy night; misery takes one lousy night. God bless you dad and all the others who suffered because of these scumbags, she spoke softly to herself.

"Calm down dear, an old friend introduced himself to let her know he is still around," the voices interrupted her. She was in no mood to be disturbed.

"How do you feel up there?" That was rather an awkward question.

Touched by an angel, she shrugged her shoulders in a rather unusual manner smoothly rolling her shawl across her shoulder blades ("Marcia Turner never did that"). She was in the league of her own.

She was setting the mood, wasn't she?

He was impressed, he had no idea who this angel was, but she was definitely manna from heaven. (From his devilish perspective)

"Ready for this?"

"What's that?" (a more, casual rather relaxed than an alarming, answer)

"A game."

"Not a game of thrones—I am tired of that—they all laughed it off. No—it is called D.I.Y. (as in do-it-yourself)"

"Do you remember that great taste you were holding?"

"How can I forget that?"

"Stop playing."

"I am not kidding, I just want you to remember, this is not child's play. We have six each."

"Yeah!"

"Ok."

"We must take all six at once. Yeah."

"And after that, it's business as usual. I mean business XXX."

He had his insulin in quick succession, and I had my H_2O in very quick agonising sessions. I enjoyed watching him enjoying it, I would say.

Oh, bless him.

The things we do for lust.

Chapter 16
The Rolling Stones

They hoped they found the breakthrough, but it was far from over. There were far too many sightings across the country, but few proved to be false alarms, but some were close calls. They were dealing with their match. Nikki's dad was a spy, not just a spy but was mastering the department. She learnt a lot from the old master.

He had a remarkable moustache, hence called whiskers, but his colleagues said they vibrate when he sensed danger or suspecting something. He was as swift as a jaguar, had a remarkable smell and six eyes. He could pick you up miles away with his facial recognition memoir and trace your tracks as if he is looking after a toddler. He was a remarkable officer. They had something in common, they were both left-handed and quick thinkers and "treated the enemy with respect," as the old master would say.

She did not have one of those catwalk style walks but had a distinctive walk. It really would take a genius to notice her from the crowd. Nikki's description was posted nationwide by this time and had a price tag on her. She could not care less. She was dancing with them. Nikki was not a socialite but was not a loner. She could make and lose friends very easily.

A s she waked down Croydon high street, she decided she has not been on the tram for a long time and after her shopping spree decided to hop on one. It was packed as usual, and the weather was permitting.

Nikki was very sensitive. She could feel when someone is looking at her and becomes very irritable when someone is glued at her. She is not a panicking type; she would gradually ease the tension by either moving away from the subject or distracting him or her and in that way making sure if she really is the target or someone is just feeding his/her curiosity She moved towards the right side of the tram and the big shadow followed. She stopped. It stopped. "Am I the person of interest here?" She asked herself. "Right, let us see what you are made of," she said, the game was on.

Nikki was a dancer and athletic. She was quick. As the tram stopped, she was off quickly and within no time into the next carriage. As the old man was still negotiating his way-out Nikki had already mingled and she was straight into the mix on the far end right corner of the tram…

"It's her, it's her," the old man shouted, chasing the tram. What is he doing? People were astonished. Why did he get off in the first place? He is so fat he cannot even walk never mind running. "He said something about stopping the tram, it's her," said the little girl to her mum.

"Oh Cherry, why are you the only one who heard that?" Her mum asked.

"Really mum," said Cherry with confidence, maybe other people heard him as well. People were minding their own business, no one was interested on that subject and pleased that there was no other audience except her was the lady in red who was listening with interest to that.

There was still some commotion at the back though as to what this old man is up to. He stopped running mum, no there he starts again. This old man is unbelievable, he is going to be very slim very soon, you should do the same.

"Run after trams, you must be joking. I am happy with my figure thank you," replied her mum.

"Can we concentrate on our journey now, leave that man alone, he knows what he is doing, Mum his briefcase flew open, he is chasing papers, have a look."

"Cherry!" That was enough to silence her. Not everyone wanted Cherry to stop as she was running commentary to the interested party who wanted to know without showing much interest where, how and when is this going to end.

Oh, no. A loud scream echoed and there was silence, followed by the heavy breaking of the vehicles. Some had their hands covering their eyes and mouths and some holding their heads.

As the old man was busy collecting his belongings that fell off his briefcase, he spotted a patrol officer across the road. I suspect the only thing in his mind was to get to him as quick as he possibly could. He ran across the road towards the on-coming traffic without even looking. That was not safe to do so.

"That's the stone rolling mum."

"That's not the atone Cherry, that is the old man rolling down the road."

"Is he? Yes, he is dead; No more questions now, let's go home."

"A rolling stone gathers no moss," muttered Nikki to herself. "I will have to google the meaning of that phrase when I am home," she said. "Let me finish my business and go home. I think that is enough for the day," she continued.

Croydon Headquarters: Emergency Briefing

"Ladies and gentlemen, I am going to be brief," said commander in chief Jacobs with a stern voice. "There have been two reported sightings today of the suspected murderer of Colonel Jones and Mr Drifoot and the latest is this gentleman who just had an unfortunate accident.

"We found in his briefcase out sketch of the suspect and the reward and the people on the tram said there was a little girl who swore that she heard the old man saying repeatedly 'stop the tram, it's her.' Now. That little girl won't make that up. This case is no public knowledge to that age yet. If only people were paying attention this could have been over by now.

"Unfortunately, we came to another dead end. Let us continue with our good work, keep your eyes and ears open.

"Let me remind you, we are dealing with a very clever calculating lady here. Do not under-estimate her, she is not scared of doing things right under our noses. Why do you think she came to Croydon today? She knows we are stretched, there is summer sale, international circus around the corner, north London derby and the launch of the new film in Leicester Square. We are scattered everywhere, there are few on the streets and there will be less officers with full streets and petty crimes going up. She has been lucky the officers on that particular street were called off to attend the thefts on the opposite street.

"She is going to slip one day. Any questions? Let us get back to work."

They dispersed.

"Bedtime," said Nikita on the other end. Some will be going home now and have their eyes wide open looking for the last-minute trophy (called luck), good luck to them. Shower, red wine and a nice movie will do me good. It has been quite an eventful day.

Chapter 17
The Christian Centre

It was an unbelievable call. The area itself had a very good reputation. It was called a holy place and the victim was a very known, respectable figure. I said respected figure and that is rather an understatement, he was a god with a small letter, worshipped in his own terms.

Police went in numbers as if there was a looming terrorist in the area, the community gathered as if it was his funeral service already and they were ready to pay their last respects.

A week ago…

"Mum, my sister I have a suggestion for this weekend. Why don't we go to the Christian Centre on Sunday and after the service we go to The Coco Banas to have an evening meal? How does that sound?"

"Why the Christian Centre?" Her mum asked.

"We can go to the local church and then after the sermon we can shoot off to the Coco Banas," she suggested.

"Mum, you know how busy is that place during weekends, people all over the world go there, and by the time we reach the Coco Bana's Restaurant there is not even a grass to park to car, but if we arrive early, we can park our car, go to church and after the service we walk straight to the restaurant without worrying about parking."

"Come on mum, we might meet good friends there as well and look we are going to the restaurant not tired and hungry for food. You know Auntie Jean and Mary here; they will keep you for hours gossiping, and we will go after an hour after the service is finished."

"Oh, am I gossiper now?" She asked. "I thought we were just analysing the sermon."

"No mum, but your friends are. You know that they are sharks when it comes to passing hot news," added Nikita.

"Ok, ok, Christian Centre it is, and I am not paying, you sort the gas (petrol) and you sort the restaurant and I am driving. Agreed?" She asked after the allocation.

"When is the last time you dug into your purse, mum?" Tamara asked and they laughed.

The Vicar

He liked new faces. He like to impress, and he thought he owned the world. Truth must be told he was a very likeable figure. Toying around was his hobby. When it comes to own the stage, he was a master. Ask him anything about the scripture, he will tear you to pieces with his answers, quotations, examples and not only referring to the ancient times but to the world we live in.

Whilst sitting listening to the Sunday service, Nikita would not stop to think, "Am I the only one who is aware of the dirtiness of this so-called holy man? Why are the people so quiet about this? What is blinding them?"

As if he was aware of her thoughts he kept on glancing at her as if to say, I can hear you. Their eyes met. "Do not look at me, I hate you and really hate you with passion," she muttered those word silently, with a very nice smile.

The vicar could not resist the temptation and as he was delivering the service, he was even inches close to Nikita. He definitely knows which side to butter his bread and he kept coming.

Nikita looked around and turned her focus to her family ignoring the attention. She did not want to be the centre of attraction.

He chose a wrong girl. He met his match. Nikita was three to four steps ahead. It was as if she could read his mind. As he was on the introductory phase. Nikki had already made her conclusion. He was already past tense in her thinking. She made it so easy for him, he could not believe his luck. Didn't he know that the road to hell is golden, with all the attractions and all the sweetest things in this world... People don't learn, do they?

He led the way, discreetly to the vestry and down the way to his so-called confession room Nikita followed like a sacrificial lamb, no question asked, smiling all the way as if she has been down this road before but inside, she was fuming, thinking how many innocent brothers and sisters have passed through this path seeking spiritual support and instead got abused. He is living a lush life eh, she thought inside. This must stop, and this must stop now, Nikita muttered to herself.

"You must be stressed sister, he tried to break the ice, opening a bottle of red wine. You did not even ask me if I was drinking or not," she said, smiling and keeping her composure.

"Oh no, this is a holy wine sister, it brings no harm but soothe your heart and relaxes your soul. This is the blood of the lord."

"I don't drink wine. Do you have anything, may be stronger than wine?"

They looked at each other and smiled. "Do you have anything in mind?" He asked.

"Your party, your choice," she answered.

He did not even get up his seat. He stretched his arm and reached for the cabinet and pulled a slender well-trimmed bottle of vodka.

"What is that?" Nikita asked.

"It is one of the finest I have known my entire life, he bragged. Let me see," she said.

"No, you cannot, that is not the language you use when you are going to drink this beautiful vodka. He was really getting into his gears."

"What's the correct way to approach this beauty?" Nikita asked. Taste, anyway you say it, this beauty will smile back at you. This is Chopin, named after the famous composer...He was a classic. One of the best in the world. The vicar was feeling pumped up.

"Oh yeah, I heard about him. That was before my time, my dad used to talk about him with his friends. Was he Polish or Austrian?" Nikita continued to elongate the conversation. That is a good question, I am not sure to be honest, but my educated guess will be Polish.

"Who is your father?" He asked looking very interested. "Forget about that, we are not here to discuss family trees, are we? Of course not, what's wrong with me?" He opened the bottle and poured for both of them. Nikita took a sip and thank him for introducing her to this beauty of a vodka (in actual fact she was no stranger to it as her father trained and introduced her to anything destructive or humble in this world). His glass had holes whilst hers was still intact. "She could not be rushed; gentlemen don't rush ladies."

"Do you always drink alcohol?" She asked with an inviting smile.

"With special people like you, yes, I like my guests to feel welcomed and special."

"I have never done this before," she lied. "So, you have been a bad boy and of course that puts me in the same pot as a bad girl. Pass me that marker and give me a clear paper."

"What are you going to do with that?" The vicar asked.

"You will see, sometimes my friends call me childish because I am fond of games."

"Bring it on," he was up to it. She wrote two separate papers. One read "I have been a bad boy" and the other was written in similar content, "I have been a very bad girl."

Realising that this could be a giveaway, she changed her tune. "No, this is not right," she said. "We are adults. To me it seems as if I am accusing you or patronising, if you know what I mean. You write and sign yours and I will do the same. After our meeting you take and tear yours and I will deal with mine."

"Bottoms up," she mumbled those words each and every time he toppled his glass. He looked as if he was in a rush. Nikita has been in this game before. She noticed that, she had a look in his eyes as to say what are you waiting for? He read that to and fell into the trap. Wrong move sucker, she told herself.

"Is this all for tonight? You are not a good enough entertainer, are you? We have been drinking and talking, where is the music, I am a dancing queen." She stood up and showed him what she is made of.

He took one step forward and stumbled. That was the plan, she wanted to see if the vodka has taken its toll. That was enough to gauge the progress and plan the next step.

Jackets flew, ties dropped, trousers were unceremoniously tramped down. I think animals were more disciplined than the vicar.

"Is that all we will be drinking this evening?" Nikita was pouring petrol into the fire. Another bottle surfaced. This is to bless us; his voice was becoming louder and louder. Those were his last words.

Out of nowhere, the sable came flying ripping his femoral artery, and really chopping off his genitalia. He did not know what hit him. He fell back on the sofa bleeding profusely.

"What are you doing? Who are you? What have I done to you?" He asked in quick succession but the sable did not stop.

"You devil on no description!" Nikita yelled with rage. "You do not deserve to live. You are a disgrace to God." She vanished.

Chapter 18
The Call

The quick strides, the stern voices and faces, the searching eyes of the army of police officers in different shades of uniform including the chief of police himself, meant no peaceful police march but trouble. Even could see that was not a social, peaceful call. It was not business as usual, something smelled a rat. The choir seized to sing, no one stopped them.

The atmosphere did not suite their hymns. Death visited the temple. Not just death, but the murder of their own, the forceful departure of their leader they loved. There was no need to tell the children to keep quiet, they just zipped their mouths. It was just tense. The vicious looks at the policemen said it all. There was trouble in paradise.

Who is Vicar Pederino? Exploded the chief of police. The clergymen looked at each other, dismayed. They all looked at Leon, his chief whip. "He is our leader, my lord," he answered after a long pause.

"Where is he now?" The chief continued staring at the deputy.

"He went downstairs few hours ago and is having a…" They did not give him a chance to finish his sentence. He was about to say "session" and they were already downstairs, the chief of police leading his crew. It was a synchronised boot footing down the stairs.

Jesus Christ! That echoed cross the congregation and the nearest birds flew away. It was followed by a silence as they lowered their heads with their official hats on their shoulders, paying their last respects. "Enough of that," said the chief, "this not his memorial service yet, let us move we have murder to investigate," barked the chief.

"I want the forensics here and now. Get the operator who received this call because the caller is dead and definitely was not reporting his own murder. This is not suicide, this is murder. I want to know what time was that call received and what time did the vicar die and I want this information as quickly as possible. Take Leo with you to see if he can recognise that voice and make sense out of it. If it is not Pederoni's voice, who's voice is that? This does not make any bloody sense."

The chief of police, having other mysterious murders to solve including the one of his own colleagues was really sweating under his collar. Somewhere, somehow, someone wants him to earn his money.

Meanwhile they were waiting for the forensics and other experts, some were surfing on the congregation trying to find out how much do they know about this incident, to find out if there may be possible leads.

The awaited information was received by the chief. "The estimated time of death was 13h00," announced the forensic team.

"And what time was the call made?" The chief asked.

"Around 14h30, chief, and it was from a masked voice," answered the operator who received the call.

"So, we have a manipulative, calculating murderer in our hands, ladies and gentlemen. Let us go and find him." By the physique of the vicar and the way he died, they were convinced it is a man who orchestrated this murder.

"Gentlemen and ladies, the message is clear. It does not take a genius to be aware that whoever has done this is making his intentions known and clear. This is not the message for the vicar only but he has been made a sacrificial lamb. We might be looking at a local but our focus should be global. We might be looking at close relations but let us not be blinded by this. Our eyes and ears must be wide open. Do not underestimate the offender, we are dealing with a genius and not a maniac 9hopefully). Find out why the CCTV cameras have been out of action?

"We do not know the motive, but we have a clue to what was written on the piece of paper plastered on his forehead which read, "I have been a bad boy." I want analysis of that handwriting and the possible prints on that note…"

"Sorry Chief…"

"Now what?" He snapped.

"The paper was clean as a whistle, no prints except the deceased and the hand-writing was the victim's as well."

"Gracious Lord. What the hell are we dealing with here? This was a carefully, crafted, planned murder. I first thought we are dealing with a maniac. Do not under-estimate this person. This is a genius in the making. He is going to make us run around chasing shadows. We must dig deep and leave no stones un-turned. Work as a team. Think and I really mean use your brains."

As the forensic took turned his body to look for other possible clues they discovered another mystery. The bold writing all over his back read, "To my predecessor, I have sinned, read and follow the Bible, it saves lives. Also draw your attention to the Ten Commandments, they are there for a reason."

"Mine is debatable, we will talk if you follow Pederoni's steps, you definitely know what I mean."

"This is tattooed in his body, this is a lead chief," said the other with excitement. "Look, look, it is stencilled and carefully crafted. Let us not get carried away, there is no way this has been made today. This was planned weeks and weeks ago having in mind there will be police investigations. Let us not fall in the trap. That is a pure distraction. We are noy going around looking for a tattoo engineer now. Few can follow the trend and ask few engineers across the city and beyond, give the task to the juniors so that whoever the perpetrator is can smile whilst the rest of the team is on his/her heels. Every clue nor matter how small it is, is vital to this case. Let us crack this one and it will keep all the doors open and narrow the hiding places. Good luck and God bless you all. Let us go back to work."

"They do not need invitation, do they?" The chief said those words in silence. A swarm of media officials were ready waiting in numbers outside. "Damn paparazzi," one of the chief's associates swallowed those words. The chief had no choice but to give them the scoop.

He reached forward to them and prepared to give them the news they were waiting for.

"Ladies and gentlemen, I will come straight to the point Vicar Pederoni has been murdered. We are not clear at the moment the reasons leading to this act. There is no doubt in our minds that this is an orchestrated, planned and calculated murder. Please bear and be patient with us, we have no leads at the moment. We are dealing the family and the shocked community as a whole at the moment. We will find the person who has done this. What I can you is this, offenders always leave one or two clues behind but this one left none, but I have a good if not the best team in the world. We will catch this person. Sorry I cannot answer questions at the moment, time is money. I will address the nation. Our hearts are with the Pederoni family and friends, this dedicated congregation and the community at large. I thank you all," and he dashed into the idling police car.

"Chief, chief!"

He was gone.

Chapter 19
The Breaking Point

She has done her dues. The religious side caught up with her. Nikita was no believer, which was a hard and bitter pill to swallow to her mum and those who grew up with her. She was a dedicated Sunday scholar at her younger years and taught the younger generation of her time. Was this the moment? Was this the end of the road for Nikki?

"I am tired of running, I cannot do this anymore," she sighed. I am coming home mum, I do not know when and I do not know how, but you two are going to see me very soon. That was the latest conversation with her mum as they swapped phones with the neighbour. That was the quickest ever conversation she had with her, no kisses no goodbyes. She was running out of time, and no one knew that better than her.

Nikita had no loopholes. The police knew that. They did not believe that this would happen but prayed that one day she will slip up. She knew that her mum's phone and all her associates were tapped by the police but could not care less. She was aware they were on her heels. She was in no mood to sprint nor play hide and seek. "Game over," she muttered to herself.

She knew she could not afford to stay longer on the phone and had to use different lines to speak to her family. She missed them dearly; it's been a year and a half on the road. She was homesick.

There is a difference between travelling and being hunted. When you travel the world is welcoming, explorable, fun and loads of choices and freedom, but when you are hunted the world shrinks, unenjoyable and you avoid that attention and miss that fun and never free even in your sleep. Nothing interests you but you become the person of interest. Everything looks dark and cloudy except the police.

One thing that never crossed her mind was to hand herself in to the police. She knew she has taken law into her own hands but also believed if she did not take action no one would even the so-called law. "People do not report these cases fearing to be humiliated and become a statistic instead of being helped," she said.

It's like nothing has happened, they walk freely because they know no one is going to touch them. "I am thirty-two years old now, and that Colonel has walked free as if he has not done any wrong for thirty years and nine months of my life and I am being hunted for making him pay for messing up my life and for destroying my family," tears went down her cheeks as she emphatically said those words.

She decided to take one more trip and visit her best friend and get some fresh air in Hawaii. "This is my last trip and after this I am going back home, no matter what," she said and packed her bags.

Chapter 20
Lucky Dip

He was tired mentally and physically. He had never been in such pressure in his entire life. Military training has been a gruelling and tough but not as tiring as the situation he is in with this case. Seeing how determined and hardworking he is, his superiors decided to take it on their hands to force him to take a break. Chief has never been on holiday for some time in his career. He was offered three weeks, but the stubborn chief signed only one week citing his ailing wife as the reason why he cannot stay away for much longer.

"Take your wife and disappear Chief," the young ones pressed, maybe thinking on the other end that he is the one who is bringing too much pressure on this case. He really is working 24/7 as he promised.

"That's the difference between a job and a call."

The third murder was a nail in the coffin for the chief and people were thinking when this is going to end, who will be next. There was a million-pound tag on her. She was so cool and calculating, people realised just after it has happened that it was her. She had those deceiving looks, you can fall into whatever she puts you into, that's Nikita's world, everyone plays by her rules.

The police finance department finalised all the holiday booking for the chief and his wife and they were ready for collection. The junior officer on the shift was asked to deliver them as soon as possible. The clerk asked him to run before he changed his mind—joking.

Previously the chief had a tendency of cancelling his holidays.

He chose Hawaii as his destination, the first time ever he had gone far from home, boy he really needed that break, new atmosphere, different location and fresh air. It was like a farewell in the department, but they knew they cannot relax even in his absence because wherever he was, he was thinking about this case and what were they doing. They were working but it was a bit quieter and peaceful. They wished he stay away a bit longer, but they will miss his guidance and the funny side of him.

The chief and his wife flew to Hawaii the next day in what seemed like a stress relieving holiday. His wife was happy because since this case she really never had proper attention nor a full day with her husband. Now was the time not to talk about the police department or the case.

A week is only five days because the first and the last day is just for packing but unfortunately, they do count as the holiday time. As a family they really enjoyed the break and to the chief's credit, he really switched off from work for few days, met new friends and toured Hawaii.

Chief was a swimmer. He was a champion in Police College and before he finished training, he enjoyed being the instructor of the new recruits. As the holiday was about to finish, he asked his wife if he can just go for a dip in the water. He wanted to feel the depth of Hawaiian beaches. His wife was not a keen swimmer, so she just let one go and allowed him.

"Which one are you going to, there are loads of resorts here?" His wife asked. The one I chose will be my luckiest dip and he joyfully danced away with a silly smile.

He took away in their hired red BMW X6. He had one resort in mind, he knew the name but did not know the location so had to rely on the map, so he googled it.

Fortunately for him it was not that far. He was pleased with himself that he agreed to take this holiday, he felt better and refreshed and to add more he had quality time with his wife. He did not regret refusing to take three weeks as this case was still bothering him. He felt he was going to crack it very soon, come wind, rain or sunshine.

It was one of those Hawaiian beach weathers. The beach was full of swimmers, tourists, school children, young and old. He wasted no time and joined the other water lovers and went deep into the water. He felt good and he enjoyed every bit. As much as he liked water, he did not want to overstay, thinking about his wife back in their holiday flat but something struck his attention.

That structure, that figure, that height, he rubbed his eyes and moved closer but careful not to be noticed. He wore his goggles and his straw hat; in case she recognises him. He looked further up the beach with his binoculars trying not to attract attention and suspicion. He noticed the tattoo on the right thigh. He wanted to come closer because he saw the tattoo on the woman, they saw on that CCTV footage in the Colonel's house and was curious to see if that matches that one. His chances of doing that were rather very slim.

Two young men passed him, and they too seem attracted to this young beautiful woman. They briefly stopped near her and in breaking the ice, one said oh, cute, mickey mouse, hey. He was looking at the tattoo. She swirled her shawl around and covered the tattoo and did not say a word-enough to say not interested boys go away please.

Mickey mouse, mickey mouse, he tried to recall/recollect what he saw on that CCTV footage. Mickey-mouse, I'll be damned. Lt General Napego was wearing a mickey mouse mask in the previous Distinction. "Is there a connection? Am I missing something here?" He asked himself. The more he is thinking about this the more it makes him think this is Nikita. Come on trust your instincts, he pumped himself up, trying to be more optimistic than excited.

He did not want to blow everything away, but he wanted to be sure. He did not want to embarrass himself in a foreign country as well. That was not his jurisdiction, and he could not afford to make a scene. "Who is she with, someone who can take her attention away from the outside world and concentrate on something else," he said, hoping for luck? That will give me an opportunity to check on things, he thought silently.

"Hi sweet, its time, to go," said a lady in black and orange swim-suit. "What's the rush," replied the young woman, "I am enjoying the wave action and the atmosphere around here. It's glorious, come on."

"Keep talking," prompted the chief.

"You know back home I would not be enjoying this weather. Is that why you English people are migrating in December for search of the beautiful weathers like these, come stay permanently here," she teased her, and they laughed.

The accent is English, she is definitely coming from the United Kingdom given her friends comments. I think my suspicions are correct, he concluded. I do not need her alone at this stage, this lady is more important, but I must not lose sight of Nikita. Let me go to the parking area because that is where they will be heading to, now. He was right, off they went but in the opposite direction.

"I cannot afford to lose those girls," he said. There was only one exit, he thought of cutting them off somewhere, but they were going quicker than him. He rushed to his car, fortunately it was not far off. What now! He held his hands on his head.

The left rear tyre was flat. That's the worst thing that could especially when you are planning to follow somebody.

Time was running out for the chief. There was a convoy forming to the exit and luckily for him all the exiting cars will pass through him, but the thing was, which car was she in? He cannot be peeping in every car and to make it worse he has no authority around here. A car on the opposite side reversed to pull out of the parking bay and the chief tried to direct it to the road. He was nearly hit by a motorbike trying to cut the traffic.

When he looked up, there they were in the motorbike, and he managed to scribble the number plate. What a relief, he nearly jumped with joy. This may be my lucky day, he smiled to himself and stopped when he looked at his car, he cannot go anywhere yet, the tyre needs to be changed.

He took a little longer than he expected but he was not bothered. He was thinking about his wife, how she will receive the news of how he spent his day out and his next plans. "I want to corner this girl myself," he said to himself.

"I am home!"

"Oh, there you are. Hell, love," he plastered his lips on her cheeks. "Go and change you smell of salt."

"Why are your hands dirty," she asked.

"It is a long story," said the chief.

"Come back and cut it short then, she put the kettle on whilst they chatted from a distance. Here am I, nice and fresh," he came and sat on the sofa. They had a cup of tea and biscuits and he told her the whole story.

"What are the plans now," she asked because she saw how pumped up, he was and knowing her husband she knew there was something up his sleeves.

"We are not going anywhere," he said.

"What about work? our holiday finishes in two days' time?" The wife asked.

"I am at work, do not worry about the holiday I will sort that out," said the chief. "Hello, this is Hawaii on holiday, remember," she reminded him.

"I know," he nodded.

"I really want you to get this woman and get over this case. What are your plans?" she spoke more like his partner.

"This is not going to be easy, my darling, that is why she came to a foreign country, but the department will work it out. I need to call the inspector now, firstly to extend my holiday and then the way forward," he was a man with a mission, this chief.

"Let me leave you with it then, I am going to take a very long bath," said his wife taking off her robe.

He spoke to his boss, was granted indefinite leave until the business is finished and the inspector was negotiating with the Hawaiian authorities about the case.

It was all set, and it was left for the chief to go and introduce himself with the Hawaiian team he was going to work with. He was like a school child on the first day to school. He really was looking forward to this adventure. Her mind was only set on holding her hand and take her home where she belonged. He never arrested someone on foreign soil. He was told to come around 9am and the chief was there, 8 o'clock on the dot.

He had to brief his new team because they did not have details of the case, they knew nothing about Nikita. He gave them a detailed report and was clear about his facts and the developments of the case so far. He told them what to expect and how skilful Nikita is.

They traced the motorbike, and it was registered under the name of Harold Dixon. They did not want to make waves. The next was to track Mr Dixon, hopefully he can lead the team to his girlfriend. The only thing they needed was the address of this lady.

"I have got a plan, but this has got to be done by one of you guys," said the chief. We go to Mr Dixon and tell him there is a complaint that the driver of this motorbike registered on his name nearly hit someone on the exit of the Marina Resort last Sunday and did not stop, so we want to question the driver.

"After he gave us the address of his boyfriend, I ring you, all you have to say is umm. yep, aah, thank you very much Sir I will tell Mr Dixon, he will be relieved, and switch off your phone. The next step is to apologise to Mr Dixon for wasting his time, the gentleman involved (who was nearly hit) is not pressing any charges, so let's forget about the matter—case closed and we have got what we wanted."

"Good plan, I am interested to know why not you, it will suit you because you are not from here?" The other team member asked.

Simply because, if he happens to tell her girlfriend in front of Nikita and tell her it was an English police officer that will rise suspicions and we will lose our suspect and Nikita is no dummy, believe me.

Nikita and her friend were living in a very quiet suburb. Mostly there were young adults but working class. It was a very hot day and people were scattered around their lawns and some in their swimming pools during the night cooling down before going to bed. The team had already taken their positions ready to pounce. They had a glimpse of Nikita and her friend, and they were keeping a close eye on them.

They seemed to be settling down with no intentions of going anywhere, which suite the team headed by the chief. He did not want any mistakes. There were no sirens, no blue lights, it was just a church mice's job (waiting for Amen before it pounces for the cheese)

Then the big moment came, the chief have spoken, NOW. The neighbours were astonished. They did not know where this crew came from. There were few on the roof, every exit covered by two to three policemen and every corner of the house manned. Chief knocked at the door (hard enough he did not need to tell who they were) and introduced himself. Her friend went to open the door, but Nikita stopped her.

"Why not," she was afraid.

"I'll do, I know they are looking for me," she said calmly.

She opened the door and invited the chief in. Before the chief said anything, she greeted him. "Hello Chief, did you enjoy the dip?"

"Yes indeed," replied the chief and read her, her rights and the team took her away.

Chapter 21
The Trial

Day 1

They called it the five o'clock star because it never missed five o'clock on the dot every morning. The old red cock was dubbed the starter of the city because if it was up, the whole city will be on the go. In that rainy Monday morning it continued a usual, waking up the city to the new day. They were all up because no one wanted to miss the trial of Miss Nikita Napego. They were curious to know the reasons behind those murders and if there was someone else working with her.

It was the first and hopefully the last triple murder trial in this city. The arrest of Nikita by the chief was the talk of the town. It was the chief's lucky break—some headlines said. It takes a genius to catch one—said the Sunday times as the chief was rewarded with good results this time. Salute to the Chief-the Daily Mail added to the tally. The city was divided.

Whilst there were cheers and congratulatory messages for the chief of the police to bring the suspect home for questioning, the others were sympathising with the Napego family probably due to difficulties she suffered from mental illness. At this stage it was not clear what drove her to commit those murders.

Because of the volume they were expecting the justice department moved the hearing to Court B, which had a larger capacity than the others. This case attracted a large audience world-wide as it was the first of its kind, committed by a woman picking the high-profile victims. What was more interesting that there was no violence or struggle involved in all these murders. Was there a motive behind these murders or were they done out of vengeance?

The hall was packed. The security was tight. The city has never seen so many policemen on duty as it was the case that day. There were not enough seats, and some had to settle outside. Fortunately, they were a controllable crowd. This was something this city has never seen before. It was likely people came from all walks of life to witness the history being made.

There was a deafening noise as Nikita came down the dock to face the community for the time since the death of the Colonel. She was still handcuffed because she was still seen as a risk according to the authorities, but she was not seen as danger to the community. She was looking down, her nice smile vanished and looked tired. There were two police officer on either side accompanying her and a third behind her.

Her solicitor approached the presiding judge and asked if the handcuffs can be taken off as she saw no need for them in the court and between her and the prosecutor they agreed and they were removed, much to the relief of Nikita and she nodded as a sign of appreciation and thank you to his team and both the judge and the prosecutor.

The trial commenced with the introduction of those who were in control and in charge and those who attended were informed the reason why everybody was there.

Nikita was put on the stand, and they laid the charges she was accused of and asked how she pleaded, and she pleaded not guilty. The whole house went into a shock and there were groans, grins and grinds.

All the eyes were in the judge who adjourned the case until the next morning and asked the defence and the prosecuting team in his chambers and Nikita was remanded in custody as the bail was refused. (There was no way they were going to grant her a bail after her elusive stint—they looked for her for a year and a half).

Day 2

The crowd was growing bigger and bigger. Nikita's plea attracted more curiosity and attention than ever as people were more interested into finding out how the defence reached that kind of a plea when everything seemed obvious. It was definitely not going to be a straightforward case as some people thought. The media was incensed. The world was looking on. The justice system was under a hawk's eye.

Judge Eleanor T. was presiding. The defence brought along with them Dr Pentz (the psychiatrist), who treated Nikita and Maggie (Nikita's mum), whilst the prosecuting team brought three witnesses two of them claiming to have seen the defendant.

The judge gave a nod to the defence as a sign that he is ok for him to start.

The defence called Nikita to the stand.

"Where were you on the day Colonel Jones died?" The defending lawyer asked.

Nikita: I was out dining with my family, my mum and my little sister.

Defence: Is there anyone to collaborate your story?

Nikita: Yes, my mum and the staff in the restaurant.

Defence: When did you know that Colonel Jones has died?

Nikita: On the television news at the restaurant?

Defence: How did you receive the news?

Nikita: I was as shocked as anybody else?

"Liar, liar…" Someone shouted in the crowd.

"Silence, silence," ordered the judge.

Defence: Did you kill Colonel Jones?

Nikita: I do not remember.

Defence: Thank you

Nikita had a sip of water.

The prosecutor approached the stand looking straight at her not blinking. "Whose idea was it to go out on Sunday at that particular time," he asked.

Nikita: It was the family decision.

Prosecutor: Can you be more specific please?

Nikita: My mum decided.

Prosecution: Of course, mum, quite convenient.

"Objection Your Honour," shouted the defence "Withdrawn," replied the prosecution.

Did you go near Mr Jones's residence from Friday to Sunday?

Nikita: Yes. I was there on Friday.

Prosecution: Specifically, at what time?

Nikita: Around 12pm.

Prosecution: But the Distinction does not start until 2pm, what was the rush?

Nikita: I like to be early and compose myself.

Prosecution: To compose yourself after finishing your preparations to kill Colonel Jones? Your Honour…

"Rephrase your question Mr Putco."

Prosecution: What were you doing all this time Miss Napego?

Nikita: I do not remember all but I looked around the garden and the surrounding areas.

Prosecution: Let me refresh your memory. Do you remember changing into a gardener's workwear and climbing into Colonel Jones's window and into his bedroom?

Nikita: No.

Prosecution: Do you remember swapping the Colonel's medication?

"Your Honour she said no she does not remember getting in the victim's room, how will she remember the rest," the defence chipped in.

"Your Honour, I have in my possession a CCTV footage showing Miss Napego disguised in a gardener's workwear in the bedroom of the victim swapping his medication," added Mr Putco.

"You may step down Mrs Napego," said the judge.

Let us see that CCTV footage and he adjourned the hearing until 2pm and went straight in his chambers with the two learned colleagues, side by side.

2pm...

The judge wasted no time and he put Nikita on the stand for cross examination. On the death of Mr Pascolino, the former head teacher.

Defence: Miss Napego, how did you know Mr Pascolino?

Nikita: I read from newspapers and saw on television that he was sexually abusing little girls at his school.

Defence: Did he abuse you?

Nikita: No, I had a lucky escape, but my friend did not, she sobbed.

Defence: Did you kill him?

Nikita: No, I let him go.

Defence: What do you mean by letting him go?

Nikita: When I went in there, he suffered an asthma attack and I watched him until his last breath.

Defence: So, you did not touch him?

Nikita: No, I just thought of the little girls he molested and had flashbacks of him chasing me and I froze.

Thank you, Miss Napego, No further questions.

Prosecution: You said I watched him and did not help him, you killed him.

Nikita: No, I did not.

Prosecution: Humans help each other, why did you not help him?

Nikita: He was no human being; he was a pig. (She said banging the stand)

"No further questions Your Honour," he said and went to sit down.

"We will adjourn now and resume first thing in the morning at 09h00." His hammer went down.

Chapter 22
Getting Away with Murder!

"This is not right! They all seemed to be on her side, after all she has done, killing so many people. What about their families? I am not saying this because I lost my brother. He was not clean I admit but did not deserve to have his life cut short like that by a strange, deranged woman who is revenging her own mis fortunes," sobbed Tania.

"Do not forget my sister, that she was failed by the same justice system we want justice from," said Erica.

"Come on Erica she shouldn't have taken law on her own hands," she continued to state her case.

"And then what are we doing now? Aren't we doing the same? Aren't we taking the law into our own hands, by arguing the course the trial should be taking? Erica put some weight on her argument. Let the law take its course," she levelled.

I am not happy with the developments of the case, that's all. I am not interfering, Tania showed she is still there.

There are two sides to the story and there is only one verdict delivered by only one person called the judge.

So, relax and enjoy the show, let the solicitor sweat and try every trick in the book, that is what they are paid for. If he wins, that is work well done and if he fails, we will call that fate because there is nothing we can change.

They seem to focus on her mental health, but the reality is, she knew exactly what she was doing and had it planned every step of the way, that bitch.

She is a calculating, clever bitch I agree with you but let us not forget she had her own reasons that led to these murders. Just put yourself in her shoes. What would you do?

She was justified to kill her biological father, may be, but not to run like a wild animal and kill other people who had nothing with her.

Women have been for a ride for a very long time.

You cannot smile at men, you are being seen as fancying them, why can't we just be seen as nice people?

We cannot go out and get drunk and enjoy ourselves, we are taken advantage of.

We cannot wear what we are comfortable with, we are judged as fishing them. That is the first question they will ask you before they totally humiliate you.

We cannot a man you are not happy with and fall for someone more suitable for you, you will be called names, nasty names.

Someone please give me a dick, just sew it nicely on my groin area. This thing has laws and regulations protecting it. Everything it does is 'pretty legal', screamed Erica after her short speech.

Have you ever been humiliated to ground 0, big fat 0 to an extent you really think you are nothing, just worthless?

Chapter 23
The Trial Continues...

Day 3

This case was fast becoming international news. All organisations dealing or campaigning again sexual abuse of women, young boys and girls, human rights activists and violence against women were incensed by this case. The atmosphere in this small city changed. It was not more about murder now, but human rights and women abuse. International journalists, media and other interested parties joined the party. The department of justice had to increase their numbers in securing the occasion as the influx of people buzzed in. Court B proved not to be enough as anticipated. There was more pressure to the department of justice as protests against the rights of women filled the streets of the city joined by the community at large.

Those protests delayed the start of the proceedings as the vehicles carrying the officials and the defendant had to negotiate their way past them to the court. Finally, the session began around 10h15.

As Nikita was escorted down the dock cheers went viral. She was to be cross examined about the death of MK, a renowned "predator" of young wannabe celebrities. Posters were flying, Girl Power, Way to go Nikita, No is No, Women Rights etc. were among the messages put across. There was a wry smile on the defence and a sarcastic grin on the prosecuting team.

Nikita was called on to the stand for the third time and hopefully the last. She was a bit brighter that day maybe pumped up by the crowd.

Defence: Good morning, Miss Napego.

Nikita: Good morning, Madam.

Defence: What was the relationship between you and MK?

Nikita: We never met.

Defence: What was the purpose of your visit?

Nikita: Curiosity mainly. I wanted to see what makes his victims succumb to him.

Defence: Did you find out?

Nikita: Yes, he was drugging them, spiking their drinks.

Defence: How did you find out?

Nikita: He poured me a white wine. I do not drink white wine, but I did not stop him. I excused myself and went to the bathroom. I had no reason to go to the bathroom except to give him a chance. He took the bait. He did not even notice the bathroom door was left ajar. It is after then I told him that I do not drink white wine and he came with a red one. He refused to drink it and it went down the drain.

Defence: What next?

Nikita: He came with cocaine whilst we were talking and I told him I do not like it and then he came with injectables, I think it was heroine.

Defence: Did you take it?

Nikita: No, I told him it was too early for that.

Defence: What did he do?

Nikita: He was coming uncomfortably closer to me and talking friendly as if he knew me for years, trying to touch me and promising me the world.

Defensive: Carry on.

Nikita: We played a game whereby we were going to inject ourselves until the contents are done and when we were done, I left the house.

Defence: Thank you Miss Napego. No further questions, Your Honour.

Prosecution: What did you and MK take during your so-called game?

Nikita: We took different things.

Prosecutor: Please explain to the court.

Nikita: I had water and he had insulin.

Prosecution: So, you swapped the heroine.

Nikita: Yes, I do not do drugs.

Prosecution: Thank you, no further questions, Your Honour.

Judge: You may step down Miss Napego. Court adjourned. Back at 15h00

The defence called Dr Pentz on the stand. The prosecution objected to this stance saying the defendant did not show any sign of mental instability whilst being examined. The defence argument was when she committed those crimes she was under the care of Dr Pentz and she is still under her care and the voices she suffered from had detrimental effect on her health particularly her behaviour. They decided that the doctor can give evidence.

Defence: Dr Pentz, in your opinion how do you see the defendant. Would you say she is a danger to the community?

Dr Pentz: She is a calm and quiet woman but when these voices invade, she can be a different person.

Defence: Different person, how?

Dr Pentz: They can take command and make her do things she even did not wish to do.

Defence: Thank you doctor.

Prosecution: Doctor, these voices, do they with the person all the time?

Dr Pentz: No, sometimes a bit longer.

Prosecution: So, a person is independent most of the time.

Dr Pentz: Yes

Prosecution: Thank you doctor.

The session ended. Court adjourned until the next day at 09h00.

Day 4

Closing Arguments

Defence:

My client was a bubbly girl with a bright future. She was born in a lovely and stable and respectful and respected family.

Her life was broken down by the news that the father she grew up knowing who nurtured her and undoubtedly loved her so much is not her biological father and Colonel Jones who sexually attacked her mother is her biological father. Colonel Jones abused his powers raping my client's mother, his colleague's wife.

As if that was not enough, Nikita suffered from mental illness, she was invaded by voices which we heard from Dr Pentz can change your behaviour completely and make you do things you did not intend to do, control you and command. They changed that lovely little girl. She did not control what she was doing but they were. She was scared. She did not know what would happen if she did not comply.

We heard from the testimony that she did not even touch the head teacher and could not help him as she froze and again the commands of the voices led her to visit MK.

My client is not a murderer. My client needs help to overcome these horrible voices. Fortunately, she has Dr Pentz who managed so far to treat her. Prison is not going to help her; she needs to continue with her treatment.

Thank you, she concluded and sat down giving opportunity to her learned friend to say his part.

Prosecution: Ladies and gentlemen, you heard what the colleague and the doctor has said. I will be brief. We are dealing with a clever, calculating person here who knew what she was doing. She planned and orchestrated those murders. She chose when she wanted them to die. We have seen the CCTV footage in Colonel Jones's house. She chose the day, the time and the place where her victim was going to die.

She swapped his medication on Friday and put them on Sunday when she knew that the Colonel was going to go fishing alone (he showed the judge the medication container). She did not put the deadly medication on Friday or Saturday because she knew that the house was packed, and he was among family and friends and he was going to be rescued. She knew that the Colonel was allergic to penicillin and chose that as her weapon to murder him.

She travelled to the hospital and visited the head teacher and posed as a doctor on the day he was discharged, and we know what happened next, the poor man died whilst she was watching, depriving him of oxygen.

The famous doctor again went to MK's residence and pretended to be a celebrity looking for fame and poisoned him with high doses of insulin and left him dead. This was no research, she planned to kill him. As you have heard from Dr Pentz, those voices do not stay with the person forever, so some of the decisions she made were independent. She is dangerous and should be removed from the society. Thank you.

The court adjourned and resumed the next day at 10h00 for the verdict.

Chapter 24
Sombre!

"Mama, I want him out of that charade. Out, out, out!" She through her bag on the sofa and went straight to the kitchen and fixed herself a very strong coffee.

"Why don't you go for a stiff tot of whisky, my love because you look like you have been watching a horror movie?" Her mum said with no clue what Kezia was talking about.

"What the hell are you talking about, Kezia?"

"Dad, you know what I am talking about, don't you?"

"Am I a fortune teller or a mind reader now?" Miranda replied.

"You just come in shouting, and you expect me to know what you are talking about at the click of your finger?" Miranda was not impressed.

"I am not good at guessing games. I think you know me better than that young lady."

"Mum, I am very sorry. I did not mean to be rude, but this trial is driving me crazy," said Kezia in tears. "This is all what people are talking about. The papers are full of it every f...g day.

"And guess who is on the headlines? Of course, my dad, and guess who is stressing most, us mum, us? You see groups of people talking and as soon as you come close either they keep quiet or change the subject. This is really stressing or is it only me who is feeling the heat?" Kezia was really stressing out.

"And so am I and so is your dad, Kezia. Do you think we are enjoying this publicity? We talk about this every day and wondering when it is going to finish. This is not your dad's war; he is standing in for the law."

"I know mum that is all he is going to say law, law, law. For God's sake he is not the only judge in this country. What about us as a family? Does someone out their care about us? What about us as women, mum? Will his so-called law stop being biased against women?"

"Kezia, stop! In the name of the Lord, please stop. We are talking about David and Goliath here. The only difference is, Goliath always win in this world we are living in. Men rule, men made laws and men rule the world. That is what we, women of this world are faced with. We all know this needs to stop and this need to be done as quick as possible. Don't you think your dad is aware of this? Don't you think the women of this feel the pinch? This has been going on for decades. It is not only about this case, but it has also been going on for thousands if not millions of years.

"It has to stop! We all know that, but there is always the right moment. God gave us Nelson Rholihlahla Mandela and Frederick de Klerk to end apartheid in South Africa and may be this is your dad's turn to turn the tide. Let the law take its course."

"Mum, that is a different case, all sexual offences go one way, men are always winners. Not any more my child, not anymore. Miranda hugged her stressful daughter."

As they embraced a big blue jag parked on the driveway. "That is your dad, Kezia, quickly put the kettle on."

"He is the one you should fix a tot of whisky for, don't you think?" Kezia said, joking.

"Do not say anything to him please. Let him settle first," pleaded Miranda.

Just as he entered and plastering a kiss on his wife's cheek, the door swung open.

"You (pointing at him) take yourself out of this case with immediate effect. This is a disgrace; don't you see that? Every single person in this country is talking about this and how the law of this country is so biased against women. This could ruin your career, open your eyes.

"People never change. A hello, and, how are you? would be more welcome especially when we have not seen you for almost a year Margaret said Saziso.

"Of course, people will be talking about this case. This is the news of the world, and I am the best judge in the world, don't you think my precious daughter?" He turned and gave her daughter a hug.

"May I ask you why am I under attack?" He asked.

"Do not be defensive, I am not attacking you I just do not want to be part of that. All the eyes of the world are staring at you," continued Margaret.

"They are not staring big sis; they are interested into knowing how am I going to handle this massive pressure. They want to see what I am made of. I am going, am I going to melt or crumble? Those who are just staring, let them stare and let me do my work," continued Saziso.

"Right now, I need a clear, working head. Is that the reason why everyone looks so sombre in this house? Let me tell you something. If you people are going to behave like this, you give me no choice but to look somewhere I can live and have a clear-thinking mind. This case is stressful enough to add other stressors in my already stressed body. I am not going to be put under pressure by my own family. Families are there to support each other not to tear another apart.

"I have been in this job more than 40 years and I am not going to quit at the click of anyone's finger. The department gave this case to me for a reason. They trusted me and I am not going to disappoint them and let down the whole world because of some sceptics. I was not chosen because there are no judges but because of my track record. This is a very big case I understand, and I am going to see it through.

"God is always on my side, and I trust my Lord, He will continue doing that. Now if will excuse me I have a verdict to consider. My advice to you all is, sit tight, pray for me and wish me a very good luck as I will need it. Law will prevail and God will show me the way. I had a very long day and I need a very good rest and do not forget I have a verdict to deliver in the morning."

They looked at each other in dismay.

He has always been so stubborn, like his father but in some cases, he was right, Fingers crossed I hope he is right this time, because if not, God help us all.

"Is he going to bed? Is he not having anything to eat?" A concerned, caring mother asked.

"I prepared everything as usual and made his special favourite food, dumplings but he never touches anything except fruit and drinks when preparing for a case. Let me go, may be his heart is going to melt and eat something," concluded Margaret.

"Not a chance. I know that one. Thanks for coming Margaret, at least we tried, or shall I say you tried."

Chapter 25
The Verdict

It was quiet you could hear the feather thumping on the velvet rug. Everybody was poised to hear the verdict. There were delays indoors and officials came in and out. The crowd was becoming anxious. There were so many factors that could influence the judgement both ways. The latest straw was the press conference called by Samantha, Colonel Jones's daughter.

She stated on the press conference on live television coverage, "I am a woman rights supporter and I do not condone what my father did to Lt General's family as a whole. They were a decent loving family and did not deserve that. They were family friends. He knew we spoke strongly against woman abuse. What he did is unforgettable and unforgivable. If you ask me where I stand, I will tell you this, I will run to that dock and stand by Nikita, she is my sister after all, thank you."

That left the door wide open, and the critics had something to chew. They had to get the balance right.

The flags were flying high and the protesters outside started they chants and singing. The court martial requested everyone to sit down as the officials were coming through.

The presiding judge, the Honourable Julius Snow-P welcomed the crowd and thank them all for their patience and support. He told them this has been a long and tiring week but at last they have reached the verdict. He thanked both the defence and the prosecution team for their hard work in ensuring that justice is done.

Citing mental health difficulties and advise and clarity form the medical experts, I found Miss Nikita Napego not guilty on all three counts of murder and refer her to continue her psychiatric treatment. Court adjourned.

Chapter 26
The Final Act

One man's meat is another man's poison. This is not a global warming; this is history rewritten, or shall I say history in the making? Ever heard a judge in such a big case, not national but global pressure being given a standing ovation in the court of law. Never in my 95 years. He thought he was talking to himself, but when he looked up, he was amazed to see that he had an audience, a sizeable audience. It was one of those moments when you do not realise that you have been very loud, not to the fault of your own but these things happen.

"Maybe you were on her list and she has just missed you by a whisker old man," said a drunken man, finishing his bottle of vodka. "Sorry, just joking," he added and danced away.

"Not a chance my brother, not a single chance. Let me tell you something. They are still talking about sex education as if it something they have just discovered, and now is going to be compulsory at schools from the early ages. Sex education has been here for decades. You start to wonder in which planet do these people come from?"

My mum used to tell us, "Isibhanxa masibe sinye ngexesha." In English terms that means, one fool at any one given time. That was engraved in our minds even before we understood the word girlfriend or boyfriend or when she sees that your ears are starting to vibrate, and eyes are starting to twitch. So, there you are, one is enough boys and girls, you do not have to paint the city red and be the talk of the town. The old man was fired up.

"Oh! I love life and you must live it to love it, my son. Stay away from trouble and the trouble will avoid you," he said whistling away.

"Chief, chief," shouted a uniformed officer, trying to get attention to a man in black three-piece suit.

"Not now, not now Jimmy," replied the chief and rushed off.

They seem to be a very unhappy bunch. Why are they not happy? They have done their job. They arrested the culprit and now they must leave it to the judge to make the decision. We love our policemen, they really do their work, they protect us (at least some do). People were not going anywhere. There were clusters still digesting dissecting the verdict of the judge.

There were of course divided opinions. The winner of course was the law.

Wait, wait, wait a minute. Is that not the Colonel's daughter? What is trying to do? Is she really holding a press conference? I cannot believe my eyes, continued one of the family members. Well, well, this could be interesting. Everybody rushed to the scene as if there was another famous case on the way.

"Ladies and gentlemen, I am sure you are wondering what am I doing here and why? I do not want to waste anybody's time and if I did, I apologise sincerely in advance. I have lost a father and so are other people. People have lost fathers, brothers, cousins or uncles. People have lost mothers and sisters because of the physical and emotional traumas these attacks have done to them. My father knew where I stood as far as Women Rights are concerned. I hate what he did and do not any human being could be subjected to such cruelty. I feel betrayed b my own flesh and blood.

"I wish today will be a lesson to us all that you can run, you can hide but, and a big but too, we will catch you and we will find you wherever you are because the arm of the law is very long, and it stretches everywhere. My sister Nikita did not win today but the law did. Long live Women Power. Long live. I hope this will touch the hearts of lawmakers and lawbreakers of this world equally and do the right thing as from today. This has been going far too long.

"To all these families who has lost loved ones, just take one minute of your time and ask yourselves, were they right? If your answer is No, join me and the rest of other Women Rights Activists to fight for the rights of women and bring these cruel animals to justice and rewrite these laws. Lock away these perpetrators and throw the keys deep in the Atlantic Ocean. I thank you. If you will excuse me, I had a catch up to do with my sister. Let us go, Nikki."

Conclusion

The world is an acting stage governed by different regulations, laws and ethics. But there is no law governing a No, no is no and there is no other explanation needed. You can say it differently in different languages, but the meaning is still the same. It means stop what you are doing and go away, please. There has been a sharp rise in date rapes in recent years.

Consenting to going out has been vastly confused with consenting to other activities including sexual activities. There are factors to be considered as far as consent is concerned, to name the few, age, health status and mental/psychological status.

The law must recognise how traumatic this is for all genders and act accordingly irrespective of race and hierarchy.

Glossary

Anticipate – expect or predict.

Chaos – complete disorder or confusion.

Climatise – to acclimate to a new environment.

Complex – a group or system of different things that are linked in a close or complicated way.

Curb – plans to introduce tougher measures, restraint/ or keep in check.

Daunting – seeming difficult to deal with in prospect intimidating.

Denominator – the number below a line in a vulgar fraction, a figure representing the total population in terms of which statistical values are expressed.

Detachment – the state of being objective.

Devastation – highly destructive / damaging.

Distinction – a difference or contrast between similar things.

Eager – strong venting to do or have something.

Extinguish – cause to cease to burn.

Haste – excessive speed or urgency.

Hurly – burly–busy boisterous activity.

Intense – of extreme force, degree or strength.

Inquisitive – having or showing interest, unduly curious about affairs of other people.

Inxeba lendoda alihlekwa – this originates from an old African saying of Xhosa clan meaning, "thou shall not make fun of other people's misfortunes/ mishaps. It could be you next."

Labelling – to attach a label, to assign to a category.

Loop – a shape produced by a curve that bends round and crosses itself, a structure series or process, the end of which is connected to the beginning.

Mastermind – a person with an outstanding intellect.

Predisposition – a liability or tendency to suffer from a particular condition, hold a particular attitude or act in a particular way.

Reroute – to send in a different direction.

Spectator – a person who watches an event.

Speculation – the forming of a theory or conjecture without firm evidence.

Sufferer – a person who is affected by an illness or ailment.

Vulnerable – exposed to the possibility of being attacked or harmed either physically or emotionally.

Wamthi baxu – looking at someone with vengeance, those looks that can "kill".

Wamqala ezinyaweni, wamnyuka – starting staring at a person from toes slowly to the head.

Weird – suggesting something naturally unearthly.